The Bad Dream

Jules Hoche

The Bad Dream

translated, annotated and introduced by
Brian Stableford

A Black Coat Press Book

Visit our website at www.blackcoatpress.com

ISBN 978-1-61227-904-6. First Printing. November 2019. Published by Black Coat Press, an imprint of Hollywood Comics.com, LLC, P.O. Box 17270, Encino, CA 91416. All rights reserved. Except for review purposes, no part of this book may be reproduced or transmitted in any form or by any means, electronic or mechanical, including photocopying, recording, or by any information storage and retrieval system, without permission in writing from the publisher. The stories and characters depicted in this novel are entirely fictional. Printed in the United States of America.

TABLE OF CONTENTS

Introduction

"Le Mauvais Rêve" by Jules Hoche, here translated as *The Bad Dream*, was first published as a feuilleton serial in *L'Intransigeant* in thirty episodes between 20 September 1923 and 20 October 1923 (skipping the 19 October issue). It was not reprinted in book form, and nor was the last of the author's several ventures into speculative fiction, also published as a feuilleton in *L'Intransigeant*, "Le Sidérateur" [The Siderator—the name is that of a hypothetical new weapon], serialized between 13 May and 7 July 1925. The two short stories included in the present volume as makeweights both appeared in the illustrated Sunday supplement to *Le Petit Journal* in 1910, "Le Mannequin" (tr. as "The Mannequin") in the 23 January issue, and "L'Auto diabolique" (tr. as "The Diabolical Automobile") in the 29 May issue.

Jules Hoche was a relatively prolific author with more than twenty books to his name in addition to work never reprinted from newspapers—the full extent of which is difficult to gauge—but little biographical information was collated in his regard. He was born in 1858 in Alsace and spent most if not all of his early life in Strasbourg, where he completed his education. Although his name was then spelled Hosch, and he spoke German as well as French, he thought of himself as French, and disapproved very strongly of the annexation of Alsace by Germany following the Franco-Prussian War of 1870.

In 1917 he published a long nostalgic account of the province and its people, looking forward avidly to the possibility that it might be returned to France when the Great War ended, entitled *En Alsace reconquise*.

Although the Bibliothèque Nationale catalogue does not identify Jules Hoche as the former Jules Hosch, several recent specialist bibliographies do so, and the attribution is undoubtedly correct. His first book—the only one he published under his original signature—was a collection of five highly idiosyncratic stories entitled *Folles amours* [Crazy Amours] (1878; three stories tr. as appendices to *The Maker of Men and His Formula*), gathered under the general rubric of *contes pathologiques* [pathological tales]. They demonstrate the author's fervent, but somewhat skeptical, interest in the scientific perspective, and a wry and jaundiced attitude to the subject of amour, which he characterized there, and in several of his later books, as a species of mental aberration in itself, and a rich source of peculiar neuroses.

The author Frenchified the spelling of his surname when his student days concluded and he went to Paris to obtain work as a journalist—a career he followed throughout his working life. His first book under the Hoche signature, *Parisiens chez eux* [Parisians at Home] (1883), was based on interviews he did with various notable individuals—including Jules Verne—in which he paid special attention to their domestic surroundings, attempting to use décor as a guide to character. His first novel, *Le Vice sentimental* [The Sentimental Vice] (1885), is a study of amour more anthropological than psychopathological, but no less ambivalent than the stories in his earlier collection.

From then on, Hoche published both fiction and non-fiction on a regular basis. *Parisiens chez eux* was successful, reprinted several times, and his next non-fiction book, a travelogue-cum-anthropological study of Palestine and Syria, *Le Pays des Croisades* [The Land of Crusades] (1885)—distantly echoed in the plot of "Le Mauvais rêve"—also seems to have done well, but his fiction never seems to have caught on to the same extent.

The most successful of all his books was *Bismarck intime* (1898; tr. as *Bismarck at Home*), which offered a distinctly irreverent account of the great man. The similarly light-hearted *L'Empereur Guillaume II intime* [Emperor Wilhelm II in Private] (1906) might have done as well had its long-term appeal not suffered somewhat, understandably, from the effects of the deteriorating political situation that led to Great War.

Hoche first tried his hand at feuilleton fiction in the 1880s, but the extent of his dabbling is difficult to ascertain; one early serial of which a mention survives, "La Faubourgienne" [approximately, The Slum Girl] (*L'Événement*, 1887), was not reprinted under that title, and perhaps not at all, although there is a possibility that it is the same work listed as *La Fiancée du trapèze* [presumably The Bride of the Trapeze] (1887). He maintained his ambition to produce more reputable work in the moderately pretentious *Confessions d'un homme de lettres* [Confessions of a Man of Letters] (1890), but there was a gap in his production after *La Vie romanesque, Féfée* [The Romantic Life, Féfée] (1892), and it was not until after the turn of the century that he suddenly became prolific as a writer of fiction, his preoccupation with the perversities of amorous attraction being elaborately displayed in a cluster of novels, some of which he grouped under the collective rubric *Moeurs d'exception* [Exceptional Mores].

The sequence began with *Saint Lazare, roman social* (1901), a study of the prison to which the prostitutes of Paris were sent when they violated the regulations then imposed on their profession, and the anthropologically-inclined *Chez les îlotes, amours extra-sociales* [Among the Helots; Extrasocial Amours] (1902); it continued with *Le Vice mortel* [The Mortal Vice] (1903), *La Carrière de Lucette* [Lucette's Career] (1903), *La Corruptrice* [The Corruptress] (1904), and *Le Mauvais baiser* [The Evil Kiss] (1905). The photographic essay *Mes 5 femmes, essai de polygamie* [My Five Wives; an Essay in Polygamy] (1905) might be regarded as an eccentric extension of the set.

Following on directly from that cluster, *Le Faiseur d'hommes et sa formule* (1906; tr. as *The Maker of Men and His Formula*)[1] must have seemed a radical departure for Hoche, although it appeared at a time when several other notable novels, wholly or partly inspired by Henri Davray's translations of H. G. Wells, were published in Paris, including André Couvreur's *Caresco surhomme* (1904; tr. as *Caresco, Superman*),[2] Arnould Galopin's *Le Docteur Oméga* (1906; tr. as *Doctor Omega*),[3] Charles Derennes' *Le Peuple du pôle* (1907; tr. as *The People of the Pole*)[4] and Maurice Renard's *Le Docteur Lerne, sous-dieu* (1907; tr. as *Doctor Lerne, Subgod*),[5] all of which were similarly penned by writers who had no sig-

---

[1] Black Coat Press, ISBN 978-1-61227-426-3.
[2] Black Coat Press, ISBN 978-1-61227-254-2.
[3] Black Coat Press, ISBN 978-0-974071-11-4.
[4] Black Coat Press, ISBN 978-1-934543-39-9.
[5] Black Coat Press, ISBN 978-1-935558-15-6.

nificant track record in the writing of speculative fiction. Hoche, at least, was returning to imaginative territory he had began to explore thirty years before, in some of the stories in *Folles amours*, although it is probable that nobody knew that except him. *Le Faiseur d'hommes et sa formule* is one of the most striking works in the set, and it is difficult to understand why it fell into a greater obscurity than the others.

Like Couvreur, Galopin and Renard, once he had started experimenting with what Renard called "scientific marvel fiction"—in order to distinguish it from Vernian *roman scientifique*—Hoche was evidently keen to continue, and the list of books by the author included in the preliminary matter of *Le Faiseur d'hommes et sa formule* lists as "sous presse" *Les Bouleverseurs du monde* [The Disruptors of the World] (1906), which appeared in two parts in a serial publication entitled *Le Monde Moderne* before being reprinted in volume form as *Le Secret des Paterson* [The Patersons' Secret] (1911); the story is a greatly elaborated and geographically-transplanted version of the basic theme of the comedy "Meister Fult" (tr. as "Master Fult") from *Folles Amours*, which, although recast as a thriller, retains a farcical adaptation of the balcony scene from Romeo and Juliet featured in the original.

Les Bouleverseurs du monde was followed by a twenty-episode part-work bearing the collective title *Gil Dax, Empereur des Airs* [Gil Dax, Emperor of the Air], aimed at younger readers, representing a considerable move downmarket from the earlier work. Similar fates overtook Couvreur, Galopin and Renard, all of whom had evident difficulty marketing scientific marvel fiction and had to adapt their ventures in the genre to the obscure fringes of the literary marketplace in order to continue publishing it. The two short stories reprinted here are evident hackwork, albeit typically eccentric; it is possible that "L'Automobile diabolique" is a fragment escaped from *Gil Dax*, featuring the quixotic aged scientist whose inventions are employed by the hero; if not, it is clearly a fragment of a similar story, extremely incomplete in itself.

The book that followed *Le Secret des Paterson* from the same publisher, *Le Mort volant* [The Flying Dead Man] (feuilleton version 1912; 1913), is an exotic crime novel in which the speculative elements are marginal; it was followed in its turn by an adventure story in which an element of scientific marvel fiction—a form of television—plays a slightly more pivotal role, *Le Roman de la chambre obscure* [The Romance of the Dark Room] (1914; reprinted in a cheap edition in 1922 as "L'Image merveilleuse" [The Marvelous Image]).

That pattern suggests that Hoche had such difficulty publishing speculative fiction that he almost gave it up, and in that regard, his career followed a similar pattern to Maurice Renard, who had enormous difficulty publishing several speculative works of speculative fiction begun before the Great War; he eventually managed to publish versions of some of them, recasting them as thrillers with a mystery element, but he mostly settled for producing feuilleton fiction in various subgenres of crime fiction. Hoche did exactly the same, but like Renard, he evidently retained a certain affection for speculative fiction, and probably recycled elements from earlier writings in his feuilleton fiction, including "Le Mauvais rêve," which gives every indication of being a patchwork, perhaps based on a story first written in 1913.

The Great War inevitably provided Hoche with abundant journalistic work, while putting a damper on his publications in book form, but he seems to have continued to write fiction, and when circumstances eased, he succeeded in publishing the novels *Premier Amour* [First Love] (1917) and *Le Mannequin de cire* [The Wax Doll] (1918), as well as the celebration of Alsace; he published *Filles d'Alsace* [Daughters of Alsace] (1919), *Fédora* (1919), and *Il faut aimer* [Love is Necessary] (1919) in a rush once the war was over.

He published a further handful of novels in book form before his death in 1926, including *Le Maquis sentimental* [presumably, Sentiment in Hiding] (1922); a thriller involving hypnosis, *L'Effarante aventure* [The Frightening Adventure] (1923); *L'Étrange imposture* [The Strange Imposture] (1923), and *Floria, orpheline de guerre* [Floria, War Orphan] (1925).

Little information is available is available about these novels, issued in cheap ephemeral formats, but that very obscurity, and the fact that the one traceable review of *L'Effarante aventure* describes it as "dangerous for weak imaginations and utterly vain for others" suggests that the author's slide downmarket had continued all the way to the bottom.

Le Faiseur d'hommes et sa formule marked the peak of his achievement, so far as his fiction was concerned, and demonstrates clearly that he might well have made important contributions to the field of scientific marvel fiction had the marketplace offered him any encouragement. "Le Mauvais rêve" is not an entirely satisfactory work, but it does demonstrate a stubbornness in the face of adversity of which aficionados of speculative fiction are bound to approve.

The speculative motif featured in "Le Mauvais rêve"—the possibility of suspended animation achieved by means of refrigeration—had a substantial literary history in works of fantasy such as W. Clark Russell's *The Frozen Pirate* (1877), although the most famous *roman scientifique* dealing with suspended animation, Edmond About's *L'Homme à l'oreille cassée* (feuilleton 1861; book 1862; tr. as *The Man with the Broken Ear*), features dehydration rather than cryopreservation.

Hoche's depiction of a technology of suspended animation is however, much closer in spirit and speculative technological depiction to modern development in "cryonics" than anything that had gone before, and it deserves to be reckoned a significant precursor of the many modern works featuring that theme. Ironically, the story seems to have been inspired by a newspaper report that hindsight informs us must have been a hoax, as observed in the relevant footnote appended to the text, but that does not detract from its claims to foresight.

Like many *feuilleton* narratives, the final phase of the story is abrupt and rather summary, perhaps signifying that the author was instructed by the editor of the newspaper to bring it to a swift conclusion—a fate to which writers of daily serials were always vulnerable, if reader reaction was insufficiently positive—and the narrative voice's continual switching from past to present tense, although a common feature of French popular fiction of the time, seems unusually clumsy and arbitrary, giving the impression that the author simply forgot on occasion which tense he was using. Further flaws appear to have been introduced into the text by the typesetter, who clearly had difficulty reading the author's handwriting on occasion, and often stumbled over unfamiliar words; some of his misconstructions might well have survived into the present translation, although the most glaring have been corrected. On the whole, however, such minor defects do not detract from the readability or the interest of the story, which is certainly more than a mere historical curiosity.

In spite of his marginality, Jules Hoche is undoubtedly one of the more interesting writers who dabbled in speculative fiction in the first quarter of the twentieth century, and he does not deserve the total neglect into which his work has fallen. He was a genuinely original thinker, both in his inventions and his attitudes, and never failed to produce food for thought even in his most casual works, although one cannot help but regret that the author of *Folles Amours* and *Le Faiseur d'hommes et sa formule* was gradually strangled by the relentless dullness of the popular demand to which, as a good journalist, he felt obliged to respond.

This translation was made from the copies of the relevant issues of *L'Intransigeant* reproduced on the Bibliothèque Nationale's *gallica* website.

Brian Stableford

THE BAD DREAM

I

At the troubled moment when a secret presentiment warned me that I was about to begin the most extraordinary adventure of my life, and when I dared to write down my impressions, not so much to analyze them as to assure myself of their rigorous objectivity. I regretted being ignorant of the art of writing.

Not that I don't know French. I know it too well, hence my disdain for the artifices of form, the rhetorical jugglery by means of which professionals liberate themselves so easily from syntax, not to say grammar.

To begin with, my momentary impressions are oscillating between the stagnation of the worst nostalgia and I know not what amused curiosity, which is suspicious of itself.

The oscillation exists, I'm sure, because it is intimately confounded with the pitching of the yacht that is taking me across the Mediterranean, a movement accentuated on the poop deck where I have taken refuge with my multiple perplexities since we lost sight of the land of France.

Where are we going?

I don't know—or rather, I only know vaguely, and, in any case, experience has taught me that it's necessary not to situate true stories in too precise a fashion.

All that I know is that we're heading toward the beautiful and flourishing city of Spalatrina, which a group of millionaires—American, as usual—have caused to surge forth entirely in a matter of years at an exceptionally chaotic and desolate point on the Syrian coast. Today it is a little land of luxury and dream, at the same time as a climacteric station much sought after by cosmopolitan neuropaths.

Except for a few private houses, Spalatrina consists mostly of beautiful promenades, spacious and admirably green parks where no one walks, the brightest of the winter visitors and holidaymakers going to ground in the sanitaria, palaces and family hotels scattered at the summit of the hill six or seven hundred meters above the level of the strand.

But it's necessary for me to explain first why I'm sailing to Spalatrina, under the tutelage of the owner of the yacht, my friend Gil d'Ax.

You might remember that Gil d'Ax is the amateur scientist whose audacious biological theories caused such a stir in Parisian intellectual circles nine or ten years ago.[6]

It's neither by virtue of an inclination for the sciences and their obscurity, nor a taste for adventures, that I'm part of his retinue at present. The truth is that I might never have quit Paris if the odious denouement of

---

[6] This character is presumably not the same person as the hero of Hoche's part-work *Gil Dax, Empereur des airs*. As noted in the introduction, however, it is probable that the present story is a belated adaptation of a story written in that period, given that its references to the recent invention of aviation would be direly anachronistic if the story were set after the Great War, but not if they were penned in the era when Gil Dax set out to conquer the empire of the air.

a marriage hadn't suddenly made me the most lamentable of human wrecks.

My wife, whom I adored, deceived me after scarcely a year of common life. We divorced, for we were both too well-educated to lend ourselves to any vile patch-up. I fell ill with chagrin, ruminating impressions of broken charm, a decisive veil drawn over life, and irremediable disgrace. Rich, liking society and its pleasures, intoxicated by the healthy ardor of my nearly thirty years, I had not understood until then that there are sad, unhappy people, and that one can die. And then, in less than a few days, a woman took away my *joie de vivre* in the pleats of her skirt: the separation "that gives a kind of foretaste of death,"[7] the malady that is part of its approaching toil, floored me. No, I would never have believed that one can suffer mentally to that degree, that one can support life with a soul as crippled and devastated as mine.

My depression was soon complicated by singular and disturbing phobias. In the bosom of a crowd I experienced a horripilation bordering on a fit of furious madness, even if the crowd appeared to me to be mostly composed of sympathetic individuals. Furthermore, the sympathetic individuals ceased to be so as soon as they approached me, and such individuals to whom I was forced to address speech incited me to grimaces of disgust; others, with the faces of women, agitated me to the point that, as soon as I was alone, it was sufficient for me to see them again in imagination to shed torrents of tears. It was then that my friend Gil d'Ax took pity on me, and it is to his intervention that I owe the fact that I am heading today toward the Mediterranean Orient.

---

[7] Author's reference "Schopenhauer."

"Spalatrina," Gil d'Ax said to me, "is the ideal refuge for the wounded and convalescents of social life. In normal circumstances your mental acclimation would be the affair of a few days. Assuming the worst, if you don't adapt, you'll still return to us cured, for the pure sky and the adorable and marvelous climate of the region reckon with the most inveterate neurasthenias.

No serious objection occurred to me, except that nature, for once, had taken the liberty of situating the remedy a long way from the evil, but Gil d'Ax had an answer for everything.

"All Promised Lands are at prodigious distances, otherwise they'd quickly ceased to be Promised Lands."

II

Everyone aboard knows one another and salutes one another by hand—one would think them a vast family—an agreeable sensation and very restful, only afflicting for a newcomer like me. And I won't be one for long, for if I don't know all the friends the Gil d'Ax's yacht is transporting at the same time as me—many have been ill since the departure from Candia—my friend has promised me that my relations will be as smooth as oil once we land, because he will introduce me himself, successively, to all the people I indicate to him.

"I don't ask as much," I replied to that offer, "and for the moment I simply want to be informed about the ins and outs of a certain young woman or pretty lady, very brunette, accompanying a elderly couple, doubtless her parents, for she's spent almost all the crossing in their cabin caring for them, so I've only caught glimpses of her."

"Always women!" mocked Gil d'Ax. "I regret, however, not being able to satisfy your curiosity; the old couple and the young woman are unknown to me, very rich Italians I think. They were recommended to me by my friend Saint-Marceau, the novelist who is holidaying in Spalatrina at present with his wife and daughter. Furthermore, a young man is also accompanying those people, the beauty's brother, I believe."

"That detail had escaped me," I was about to reply, but the preparations for mooring and disembarkation interrupted our conversation, and from then on it was the landscape that required all my attention and that of my dog—for I have brought that comrade of my last five years, and I shall introduce him when the time comes.

Prevalent in the disorderly pell-mell of my first impressions, for the moment, are the prestigious plumes of the palm trees girdling the beach so sumptuously, the bold and seductive costumes of strolling women, and two hydroplanes posed at the end of a wharf like two giant seagulls alighted there. Then too, there is an emotion that is restful for a Parisian like me: no face or gaze reflects the slightest material care, and that is sufficient to create an atmosphere of security and pace, which my feverish being, ordinarily so tremulous, inhales with intoxication.

Come on, it's already necessary to decant.

"You're lucky," Gil d'Ax says to me as we're having lunch at the Libyan Palace, where I'm staying temporarily. "Whereas, the other side of the coin, the days and nights in Spalatrina ordinarily go by with a dreary monotony, extraordinarily, a mystery—a word that doesn't have meaning in these latitudes—is polarizing all imaginations at present.

"Oh dear," I said, pulling a face sincerely. "I would gladly have done without here the condiments that one is obliged to abuse in Old Europe."

"Wait, though; the mystery in question offers extraordinary aspects and has nothing in common with the gossip and scandal of which we habitually make a meal in Paris. It's a matter of a fellow who seems to have fallen from the Moon, all the more so as his apartment has been retained by Simpson's by telephone. No one knows where he's come from, in fact, since no steamer has moored in the harbor for a week.

"Where can he have come from? That's the question that is haunting all brains, and it's all the more logical because he not only doesn't seem to know himself, but doesn't even know where he is at present.

"In addition to the fact that he appears to have an almost derisory debility, with a greenish complexion, glaucous and glacial, it's said—glacial, at any rate, for all those who observe him—his brain offers bizarre lacunae. Certain words already old, which are employed currently throughout the world, seem completely unknown to him, such as the words autobus, airplane and, in general, all the new words forged by aviation, of the advent of which he seems completely ignorant, although he seems to be intelligent, speaking English and French perfectly. A typical detail: on perceiving the two hydroplanes moored in the harbor, he asked what those machines could be, and when someone replied that they fly in the air, he shrugged his shoulders with an incredulous and disdainful smile."

"Perhaps he's simply mad," I suggested.

"Pardon me!" said Gil d'Ax, laughing. "If he were mad he'd already have found a means of joining the Undesirables Club."

"Pardon me in my turn," I put in, "but what's that?"

"A circle of excessively rich men, multimillionaires, who have been baptized by antiphrasis the Undesirables, perhaps also because they're only tolerable to one another, and unless one is in their sphere one has every interest in not knowing them."

And we talked about something else; as we were about to separate, however, Gil d'Ax gave me a pamphlet, a sort of geographical and administrative guide to the country, which, he said, would facilitate my natural and social adaptation.

Left alone, I circled my hotel room like a lion in a cage. I suddenly had the irritating sentiment of a disapproval of my entire person, the sensation of physical embarrassment and latent anguish that grips you in new environments foreign to your intimate being, a sensation that is only the reaction to the mental disturbance that accompanies any labor of adaptation.

And then, an adorable silhouette of a brunette Madonna is haunting my imagination, and I suddenly remember that, since the awakening of my sentimental life, I have always applied the maxim of I no longer know what La Rochefoucauld: "There are individuals who can only be cured of one woman by another."

Then again, there is the inevitable fit of preventive jealousy: "Yes, but what about the young man who is surely part of her intimate entourage?"

It only remains for me to walk to the abode of Saint-Marceau, the relative responsible, according to Gil d'Ax, for the beautiful Italian whose image has gradually laid siege to all the districts of my consciousness.

III

Thanks to Saint-Marceau, I am almost informed now about my unknown brunette.

Her name is Gilberte, Gilberte Riviez-Banchi. She's French, originally from Nice, but adopted by an Italian couple, the Banchis, him a septuagenarian, her aged about sixty, possessors of a great industrial fortune that they edified conjointly in Louisville, in the United States. Gilberte's mother was the governess of the Banchis' only child, a girl who died of phthisis at the age of seventeen. Inconsolable, the industrialist and his wife authorized Madame Riviez to send them her own daughter, Gilberte, who was twelve, who won the hearts of the Italian couple and was adopted by them a few years later when her mother perished in a railway accident.

The continuation of her story involves a great disappointment for me. She is betrothed, engaged to a man who disappeared five years ago without leaving any trace or clue susceptible of aiding those whose have searched for him, or giving any idea as to his fate.

The Banchis had two nephews, also orphans, Antonio and Giuseppe, the former six years older than the latter. Both were born in Louisville, where their father, associated with old Banchi, his brother, had quarreled with him and was financially ruined; they had been brought up by the care of their uncle and then sent to New York in order to make a situation there.

Antonio succeeded brilliantly, and as his position as an engineer facilitated voyages, he often returned to the hearth of the uncle, who had not yet thought of quitting Ohio. It is thus that he became smitten with Gilberte, who had reached the age of sixteen; he was over thirty. The old Banchis consented to the engagement, with the reservation that they should remain the sole judges of the time when the marriage could take place; Gilberte's health, profoundly afflicted by the cruel mourning that had struck her in adolescence, was extremely delicate.

Nine or ten months went by, during which Antonio remained with the Banchis. He was always extremely attentive to Gilberte, but his character deteriorated gradually. He became morose and anxious, an extreme nervousness alternating with profound prostrations with no apparent cause. Old Banchi suspected morphinomania, but could never convince himself of it. He had instituted Antonio as his legal heir, on condition that he recognized as a dowry to his wife half of the fortune that reverted to him by the fact. The younger brother, Giuseppe, by contrast, was almost disinherited, his deplorable conduct in New York having alienated the sympathy of his uncle and guardian.

On the day when Antonio reached his thirty-third year, he approached his uncle again in order to ask him to consent to his immediate marriage to Gilberte. Either out of egotism, or because he deduced from the neutrality, scrupulousness and deference of his adoptive daughter that she was in no hurry to be separated from them, old Banchi brought out once more the dilatory pretexts that he had invoked to the betrothal—and there was a rupture.

Antonio left Louisville furtively a few days later, leaving an incoherent letter in his room in which he said, in substance, that he was going to disappear from America and everywhere, and would doubtless never be seen again, unless, impossibly, he survived the proofs that he would impose on himself in order to render himself worthy of the person who had disdained him, for the sole apparent reason that she judged him to be too old.

In fact, like the majority of specimens of the southern race, Antonio seemed much older than his age, while Gilberte, whose mother was from northern France, still had the false appearance at that time of a little girl. The pretext invoked by him for disappearing was nevertheless unjust, for there had never been any question between them of the difference in their ages, Antonio's increasingly concentrated and hermetic turn of mind having ended up banishing all intimate and personal matters from their conversation.

Four years passed, during which the Banchis, having returned to Europe, at least had the satisfaction of seeing Giuseppe, the younger of their nephews—the survivor, one might say—recover morally and materially. Antonio, having disappeared from everywhere as completely and definitively as if he were dead—and doubtless he was—had bequeathed to his brother the succession of his personal enterprises, and that alone had sufficed to regenerate him, raise him up in his own eyes and restore his human dignity. Deprived of all energy when it was a matter of making a place in the sun for himself, he had adapted admirably to a ready-made situation, extracting himself at a stroke from the material rut in which he was bogged down.

Thus, eighteen months before, he had reappeared in the Banchis' house in Candia, where they were on vacation, repentant and wiser, a prodigal son pardoned in advance, since he was furnished with all the proofs of a striking rehabilitation due to his own efforts.

The flood of information furnished by Saint-Marceau having poured for a quarter of an hour over my fragile attention, I perceived, not without shame, that I was no longer listening; my curiosity had gone off at a tangent, as often happens to me, and I was floating above it, detailing its sad booty, and observing baroque coincidences that no one had thought of noticing.

I am not proud, no, of course not! I think about her with a sort of distress. I see again her magnificent eyes, her profound, ardent, emotional eyes, flowers of mourning and sunlight blooming amid the silky fringes of her mantilla.

Such as I had glimpsed her on the deck of the yacht, outside any social or familial ambience, she belonged to me; yes, she ought to have belonged to the first person who would love her gaze…but it was too late. The silhouettes of two men were profiled in the sensitive mirror of her intimate being, Antonio, who had disappeared five years ago, and Giuseppe, Antonio's brother, who was perhaps thinking today of simply substituting himself for his brother.

In fact, is he only thinking about it, or has he already accomplished it?

Warm shudders run through me at the idea that I had stupidly forgotten to ask that question of Saint-Marceau; a mist pearls on my face; I take out my handkerchief...hold on, where's my wallet?…oh well, as they say in the regiment.

A moment later, I feel my elbow nudged lightly.

"Excuse me, sir," said the voice of a man, "I called to you, but you didn't hear. You've just dropped your wallet."

Damn! There are bonds in that wallet, wads of cash, a few checks made out to the bearer, almost a small fortune.

I thank the stranger, a young man with a mat complexion and a slightly hooked nose, who bows, smiling. If he didn't have heavy and timid eyes, one of those gazes over which the eyelids settle with a deplorable facility, he would produce an entirely good impression in me. He is, in any case, very sympathetic, very correct, and his smile and his manner, like his garments, are impeccable tailored, as in a doer of good.

"To whom do I have the honor…?"

He hands me a card in exchange for his own, and when he has finished pivoting on his heel I read: *Giuseppe Banchi.*

This time I do not lose my presence of mind; I immobilize the young man with a very affable exclamation: "Haven't we just traveled together aboard the yacht *Iris*?"

"Yes, except that I can't tolerate the sea and never cease to be frightfully ill from the beginning of a crossing to the end, so I only showed myself on deck once; otherwise I would have been glad to make your acquaintance, Monsieur d'Autremont. But we'll certainly have the opportunity to see one another here."

"I'll contrive it, if necessary, if only to thank you once again."

With that, Giuseppe Banchi withdraws discreetly, like a man forbidding himself to confront the expression of my gratitude any longer.

IV

The following day I rented an Italian house, a little cubic awning in fine stone half way up the cliff, ornamented by a veranda with a colonnade, buried under rose-bushes, daturas, white or violet nightshades, with a palm tree or a fig tree at each corner. That evening, at the hour when dusk draws its crepe over the magic of a sky of apotheosis, on the threshold of the first night to pass in the bosom of an unknown world and an agglomeration of individuals solely consecrated to idleness and dreams, I experienced the delightful, intoxicating sensation, also spiced with a hint of anguish, of someone to whom it is given to recommence his life...

This morning, I encountered Gilberte near the Main Bridge; she was accompanied by Mademoiselle Suzanne Saint-Marceau, the novelist's daughter.

Here I attract the attention of those who read me to the insensible, unapparent, often unperceived fashion in which we enter into contact with individuals or events that are to have a durable and powerfully resounding effect on our existence. Mademoiselle Gilberte, I did not know a few days previously. Yesterday, her eyes moved me. Today her smile, admirably candid, bowls me over and fascinates me. Tomorrow, I shall be unable to bear the idea of being far away from her. And then, God alone knows where it will end. Strong-willed individuals sweep aside these contingencies; personally, I cannot.

That is because the elegiac Gilberte appears to me as a somber and prestigious drama in the midst of the insipid vaudeville of so many existences, all repose and gilded in slices. She bears in the mourning sky of her eyes all the gods of dream, illusion and suffering, all the tender or grim divinities that doubtless presided over her mother's destiny. And I love that she is so dissimilar to the happy and triumphant young women who embellish the milieux that I have frequented for too long.

Yes, I love her, in spite of the fact that I don't know her at all. And it isn't only the secret drama of her life that I love, it's her in her entirety, or at least the little that I've seen of her: her smile, her gaze, a little of her forehead with dark curls—an ivory trefoil cut out in festoons of jet—the tea-rose pallor of her face, and her black dress, whose pleats evoke the shade, which is also dear to me, of her dead mother.

Henner has painted those young women, in whom the appearance of mourning symbolizes a dying ideal, a prayer that does not know in which Heaven to take refuge.

Make no mistake: I love her without any troubling hidden agenda, with a pious and tender fervor that appears to me to be negative of all desire. I love her as I remember having loved a little sister carried off by typhus at the age of ten, as I have loved other little girls whose meager and precious gestures, coaxing faces, fertile in smiles or tears, ornamented the dreams of my childhood.

V

I have analyzed myself carefully, but I can't make out very well what is happening within me. It seems that the dear image that has invaded my being has remade an absurd virginity of heart and mind for me.

I am recovering the modesties and timidities of old, of a past of mirage and illusion, the ragged puppets of which have been lying in the limbo of forgetfulness for a long time. Now they're waking up, and the child that held their strings is resuscitating also, ready to transform my life of a mature man into a delightful marionette theater with magical wings, in which the wind of dreams and the unreal that reigns perpetually over the enchanted edges of sentimental life is blowing again.

And what is heart-breaking, what is redoubtable, is that the child substitutes himself entirely for the man as soon as the word "Gilberte" appears, and then, dispossessed of all empire of myself, I cease to be the master of my actions. I fall back into the odious timidities of before my twenty years, preferring, like all timid individuals, the dilatory and tortuous intrigue of romantic adventure to a clear and frank explanation.

I don't talk to her in person for fear of betraying myself. I don't even question Saint-Marceau any longer; I would be necessary to confess and I can't. Even less can I confide in Gil d'Ax. He would offer me an intervention full of mocking implications.

I would rather speak to Gilberte, one to one, without any intermediary, shielded from all moral or social interference. Evidently, that isn't correct, is even contrary to the most elementary decency in a society careful to maintain, as a counterweight to a certain liberty of mores, a respect for etiquette, the elegant demands of a worldly savoir-faire. But, once again, it's the timid child who is on stage here—and also the *enfant terrible*, who needs absolutely a solution that is not watered down, not papered over by any influences.

I've sought and I've found the most stupidly classical means, which served the isolates of the old world, all those who had no other possible theater than the street; I find myself in her passage every day, in the Main Bridge, and as I've acquired the habit of saluting her because of the intermittent presence of her friend Suzanne, I continue...while awaiting the indefinable incident that will fatally bring us together. For two or three days it's been evident that she expects our encounter; she responds to my salutations with a charming smile that reflects al the melancholy grace of her being, and then she lowers her eyes and an indefinable emotion contracts her hermetic features. What can she think of me?

The "follower" is a type entirely unknown here; there is no example of a man approaching a young woman or a lady to whom he has not been introduced. And that is explicable in a very civilized society, where almost everyone knows one another and in which a very American liberty of female behavior repudiates approaches in the street.

Yesterday evening, at the enchanted hour of dusk, the slightly heavy heat incited me to take the air in my belvedere. My gaze was plunging into the rutilant gulf of the sky and, from time to time, wandering along the shiny slope where the upper city is staged like an amphitheater, when suddenly, a hundred meters to the left, an empty patch of sky between the flowery balcony of a villa and the sharp ridge of the house itself was animated by a white silhouette that immediately turned to its advantage all the interest of the décor.

My heart turning over, I run for my binoculars. I was not mistaken, my presbyopic eyes had recognized the contours dear to my memory. I did not know that we were dwelling so close to one another, even closer that it appeared at first glance. As the crow flies, in fact, we are only separated by the slopes of fleecy verdure of two concentric avenues, and as our villas appear to be on the same level, the winding road that curved inwards to my left must put me within fifty meters of her.

And now I can distinguish, through the magical crystal of the binoculars, the beloved lines of the face, the mat clarity of the forehead beneath the black curls, the tender and profound gaze, so tender and so profound that I am already asking myself anxiously whether she does not love being in society too much and whether she is not too universally beloved for me to reign over her heart.

The time to turn the head and the dear face, in its turn, is half-masked by a pair of binoculars aimed at me...

She must have recognized me almost immediately, for she lowers the instrument, become unnecessary, and I distinguish the charming smile with which she recompenses my patient quotidian sentry duty on the Bridge. Then I agitate violently a scarf that is trailing within range of my hand. She disappears with a timid sign, a kind of farewell sketched by her fingertips.

And it suddenly seems to me that the hieratic gesture of the little hand lights up the sky, which is beginning to darken, miraculously.

Frightened by the idea of becoming suspect to her, and not knowing how to extract our adventure from the romantic rut where it might linger for a long time yet, I had myself introduced to the Banchis by Gil d'Ax at a concert at the Kursaal and I obtained an authorization to visit them the following day.

The old couple gave me a welcome vibrant with cordiality and urgent good grace. "We adore the French, and besides, our adopted daughter is your compatriot…etc., etc,

And she arrived; we spent a long time together, delightfully. Her admirable gaze posed upon me, closed and hesitant at first, then gradually uncovering the immense and poignant melancholy that lurks in the depths of her irises, speckled by sunlight, a sunlight in which the reflections of mortuary candles play.

There are evidently great affinities between her and me. Our voices have the same grave timbre, our emotional faculties have identical roots; so the psychological embroideries that she sews on the canvas of our dialogue inform me precisely enough of her personal concerns.

About Giuseppe, she says immediately: "A charming fellow, isn't he? But it's a miracle that he saw your wallet fall from your pocket, for he never occupies himself with others, and outside the radius of a meter he's entirely unaware of everything around him. That's how he made the entire crossing without entering into relations with a single one of the passengers on Monsieur Gil d'Ax's yacht. It's true that he can't tolerate the sea, and that it's only on the insistence of his uncle that he decided to accompany us here."

Colorless details in appearance, like the indifferent accent that renders their expression banal, but from which I conclude very rigorously that the "charming fellow" has not taken the "succession" of his vanished brother; in other words, he isn't Gilberte's fiancé. And that's a relief.

But it's my turn to speak, and naturally, I unpack everything that I know about the insipid mystery that is stimulating the curiosity and the gossip of the town, the quasi-supernatural reappearance in Spalatrina of the previously-vanished Lord Cattledown.

"For," I observe, "my friend Saint-Marceau knew this Lord Cattledown and claims that, ten years ago, he was one of the founders of Spalatrina."

Gilberte's face is more melancholy; if one can put it thus, there is more vagueness and more space in her gaze; it seems that the depressed soul of her eyes is struggling against a supreme shipwreck; doubtless I have maladroitly reawakened tender memories that link her to another disappeared individual.

"And yet," she says, quietly, "what is strange is the unexplained fashion in which Cattledown has suddenly reemerged in Spalatrina, where no ship has moored for a fortnight…not to mention his mentality, so curiously deprived, it seems."

A short silence. A sudden question presses upon my lips, which summarizes obscure mental deductions.

"Have you thought about a sojourn in Spalatrina?"

The response is affirmative, but such emotion is painted in her somber gaze that I dare not risk the two corollary questions: why and how?

I retain just enough presence of mind to change the subject of the conversation; she lends herself to that by asking me for news of my dog, whom she has encountered several times in my company. I tell her that he knows her name, having heard it pronounced twice.

"He's a briard, very intelligent and highly evolved. He understands most of the words of our language, and when someone speaks to him he has the slight inclination of the head that is the fashion of being attentive of creatures in which hearing is, like scent and sight, an essential vehicle of ideas. When he has a sudden joy, he laughs with all his teeth, his chops folded up to the nose, almost in the way that negroes laugh. He's also black-faced, save for two patches of yellow above the eyebrows. Many dogs are able to laugh, contrary to what the author of *Dingo* thinks,[8] and they're all, without exception, able to weep."

"Because in the society of man, of whom the dog is the friend, but who scarcely returns the compliment, occasions to be sad are more frequent than others."

"That's true. Flax was sad when I got him, and had been for six months. He had spent almost all of those six months chained up in a barrel in the courtyard of a farm, fed on crusts and rubbish. In general, all of that was rotten, and that alone would have ended up killing him, to the extent that he had a very strange notion of canine nourishment. For a long time he refused soft bread and fresh meat, unable to conceive that any aliments exempt from a foul taste or savor of corruption could be destined for him. Today he purrs over his plate however short of irreproachable the cooking falls."

"Have you taught him any tricks?" Gilberte asks, keenly interested.

"He's trying. He fetches things and carries out small commissions, but on my orders alone."

---

[8] Octave Mirbeau published *Dingo* in 1913.

All of a sudden, Gilbert has the air of someone following a complicated idea who has run into the difficult solution of some intimate problem.

To create a diversion I propose to introduce her to Flax one day soon. Her face brightens.

"Oh," she said, "I'd be delighted to make his intimate acquaintance at the earliest opportunity...

Monsieur and Madame Banchi reenter the stage, accompanied by Giuseppe, who comes to me holding out his hand. He is decidedly a charming little young man, neither handsome nor ugly, broad-backed, with a healthy tan, and a slightly sharp profile, but eyelids less heavy than they appear at first glance. Perhaps their artificial heaviness comes from a tic that causes him to lower his eyes too frequently, doubtless a relic of a congenital timidity. It is belied for the moment by the smiling, easy limpidity of his violet eyes, and the amiable and cheerful words that he addresses to me as if to an old acquaintance.

Yes, decidedly, he would be entirely sympathetic to me were it not for the fear of discovering in him, sooner or later, a rival.

I would swear, however, that Gilberte has no penchant for him at which there is reason to take umbrage.

VI

Well, no, this time I revolt against the slowness that continues, in this century entirely consecrated to speed, to preside over the gravest events of sentimental life.

I have never been able to temporize, to procrastinate, and I deem that dangerous corners ought to be taken at speed, the risk being abridged. Yes, it's necessary that I have a clear heart today.

And I hasten to the Saint-Marceau house.

The writer has gone out in the company of his daughter. That is fortunate, for it's to his wife alone that I intend to confide myself. I knew her well when her name was Lucette Grandier; furthermore, we're the same age, about twenty-nine, and, I'll add, of the same psychic tendency.

She too is unable to tolerate the delays that life imposes on any liquidation of the heart.

I pass my card to a Sudanese servant who introduces me a moment later into a shady boudoir as profound as the nave of a church.

Marriage has scarcely changed Lucette; she has remained the troubling and tremulous creature of old. She has the same dark blue eyes that have a vertiginous attraction, the same tragically red voluptuous mouth, the same ardent, feline hips, perhaps a little more rounded, with inflections of a more self-assured grace.

Without any oratory precaution, I tell her my situation, and immediately she interrupts me to tell me that Mademoiselle Riviez-Banchi is almost unknown to her, even though her daughter Suzanne linked herself with

Gilberte the year before, during the three months they spent in Nice.

All things being equal, does she intend to remain faithful to the memory of her vanished fiancé? On what terms is she with Giuseppe? She has never broached those subjects before Suzanne.

I was sure of it. My beautiful Gilberte is too hermetic to confide the secrets of her heart to a casual friend, especially one much younger than her. So it is not in the hope of obtaining intimate information that I am addressing myself to Lucette, but in order to beg her to make a discreet personal enquiry of Gilberte herself, in order to know, firstly, whether, in principle, the idea of marriage conflicts in her with any old sentimental dream.

My plea is naturally adorned with all sorts of propitiatory flatteries: "You're so rich in imagination, and also so practical, so overflowing with life, and hence so fascinating, so persuasive."

"Enough, enough, don't throw any more of them," said Lucette. "I'll carry out your mission immediately, and I'm sure of succeeding, but"—a flame of malicious curiosity lit up in the depths of her sapphire pupils—"if the result is conformity with your desire, is it necessary to put forward your candidacy right away?"

"Oh, certainly, for…I don't know why…I have a sort of presentiment…oh, an obscure presentiment, in which I can't discern anything that can be defined or analyzed…I have a presentiment that, perhaps in a few days, it might be too late."

Lucette shrugged her shoulders. "Bah! That presentiment resembles terribly an amorous impatience. Oh, you'll always be the same, the child who can't sleep until his broken doll has been replaced by another. No matter, I accept, but trace the limits of my role for me."

"Oh, it will be limited to informing her summarily about my past and asking her, if all goes well, for a decisive interview, under the aegis of her adoptive parents, of course."

"How you go about things! Why, in fact, not sound out the parents first?"

"No, this time I only want to owe my wife to herself this time...and in any case, I'm sure they'd refer me to her."

"You're right. Let's be precise, then: this is what I'll say to her. I'll tell her that your father, Monsieur d'Autremont, who died a few years after your mother, has left you a certain fortune, which, contrary to the custom in favor with the young men of today, you've never sought to dissipate. Living broadly on your income, you don't exercise any profession. Moreover, you're fond of art, literature and music, and that dilettantism, appropriate to all men of the world, supplemented by sport and slipping in a few romantic intrigues, appears to have been fully sufficient for your mental and physical development until the moment of your marriage. Is that exact?"

"On all points. You can simply add that before anything else, I'm a dreamer, a contemplative individual, which not only justifies my idleness but also explains my present black malady: I'm paying the ransom of all the false ideas I had regarding life, women and everything.

Lucette smiled politely, "That *mea culpa* might be held against you, but I'll pass over it in silence, and in any case, it's probable that you'll cure your black malady in this paradisal corner of the earth, where the mistakes inherent in every human destiny are reduced to a minimum. I'll finish my little notice. Two or three years ago you married; you espoused a young woman of your society. It was a marriage of mutual inclination, wasn't it?"

"I believed so, at least."

"After a few months of marriage your wife deceived you. You don't know yourself whether t went as far as sin; you discovered letters; that as sufficient for you. You deemed yourself deceived, and you divorced."

"It was my right."

"No one will contest it. One could say that, given the mores and prejudices of our society, it was your duty." After pause, Lucette added, with a delectable smile: "I think that's all I have to say, except for insinuating that, in addition, you're still a great child."

"No need; she must suspect it."

"Perfect…let's hope that she also suspects that this direct step, which only involves the adoptive parents in second place, signifies that your intentions concern her alone, outside any question of dowry."

"Your perspicacity honors me."

"I'll see her this very evening, then, and I believe I can promise you a answer tomorrow."

And that's it. It's tomorrow today, and I'm awaiting the promised response.

VII

I won't have to wait long. My valet de chambre, a superb negro, decorated like a Turkish emir, has just announced to me that a "woman" is waiting for me in the pavilion that gives access to the garden.

It's her!

I'm no more distressed than necessary. Nor is she, for she has the absolute independence of manner that the entirely American mores of Spalatrina concede to women as soon as they pass their twentieth year—and Gilberte is nearly twenty-three.

For the first time, we look deep into one another's eyes, into the depths of the soul, glad to perceive one another in our true light—which is to say, stripped of all the false reliefs lend to us by the various milieux that we have encountered before today. And it suddenly seems to me that her pretty tea-rose pallor is turning to pale lilac.

That is, no doubt about it, the passage of an emotion...of what nature? I would give my life to know, for I sense that with that frisson we have just crossed the threshold of a redoubtable and mysterious avenue, the exit of which is totally unknown to us.

I try to express the confusion in which the honor she is deigning to do me plunges me, but she cuts short almost immediately the clichéd politeness in which I'm wallowing.

"I beg you, Monsieur, to know that it's for me to apologize. Giuseppe has deposited me at your door and he will only come to collect me in an hour, because he knows that I desire to talk to you in complete intimacy, for if I've come here instead of receiving you at my adoptive parents' house it's because I have grave things to say to you, and although Giuseppe is almost acquainted with my secret, he has understood that his presence would embarrass us. He doesn't know everything, however, because he doesn't understand everything, while you, I have judged to be similar to myself...yes, I've divined in you a man speaking, by virtue of a miracle, the same language as me, that of sentiment."

Completely bowled over by the mystery included in that exordium and by the indescribable enchantment spread around her by her charming silhouette, draped in somber gauze and gloved in black to the elbows, I must have responded terribly confused things.

Certainly, she was not deceived in supposing me to have a soul similar to hers. Before intersecting, our two destinies must have known identical emotions, similar dolors and joys. We did not have the mental temperament of the caste that we represented by a pure double hazard, she having known as a preface to the fairy tale of her present life, all the suffering germinated in the humble condition of her mother, and me, raised no less simply, almost harshly, by an engineer father, the issue of the most modest social sphere, who had only realized a fortune in the declining years of his life. We could therefore extend out or hands to one another, to put in common something other than more or less tyrannical enjoyments founded on the power of gold.

"What is certain," I concluded, "is that the sentiment I experience for you is an entirely pure, entirely disinterested inclination, an inclination that, at least, will not leave me, if I die suddenly, any of the remorse with which the end of any existence is dotted. Let me tell you before anything else that I love you passionately for yourself alone, with an absolute respect for your sentimental past and a tender pity for the mourning, all the more cruel for being uncertain, suspended over the first hopes of your heart. Now, you can speak."

She is sitting on a small settee, her bust upright, suddenly very pale, her pretty as if compressed under the weight of the revelations that she is making ready.

"The uncertainty to which you allude, and which was certainly cruel, scarcely exists any longer, for I have begun to lift a corner of the veil of mystery that has surrounded the disappearance of my former fiancé Antonio until now...oh, don't go pale; I always told him that I felt a great affection for him, but not amour, otherwise I would not have accepted the indefinite postponements that our parents imposed on us. Does one know why one loves or doesn't? It's a mystery as great as life itself. But let's pass on; I owed you that confidence in order that you know"—a rapid emotion made her voice tremble—"that in not rejecting the homage of your amour, I am not betraying any oath, and I am not infidel to any memory..."

At those words I fell to my knees before the beloved and declared to her that it was my entire life that I was offering her with my name. She thanked me, and told me, blushing, that she would perhaps accept it, when she had fulfilled all her duty toward the disappeared individual. Her voice immediately became melancholy, as if distant.

"He too, alas, offered me all his life, and it was perhaps because I seemed to be disdaining his offer, yes, perhaps it was for that reason, that he wanted to disappear. You will understand, therefore, that before pledging my faith to you I intend to find him and to obtain his pardon."

"Find him!" I cried, with the sensation that my dearly beloved was sacrificing to an exaggerated scruple in subordinating our happiness to the deciphering of an insoluble enigma. "Do you suppose, then, that he is still alive?"

"I'm almost sure of it."

"Then you have some indication…a trail to follow?"

"Yes, and that's exactly what I want to talk to you about, for we're convinced, Giuseppe and I, that you can be a great help to us in the pursuit of our enquiry. Whereas people would mistrust him because he is the brother, a stranger will not awaken any suspicion, and will at least disarm essential mistrust. Wait, and you'll understand, because I'm going to confide to you now things that I haven't imparted to anyone, except Giuseppe, and which will remain between us. Antonio had, in a way, prepared me for his disappearance. He had an unquiet mind, inclined to black ideas, tormented by a thousand phobias, as the physicians put it."

"It has been affirmed since that he was a morphine addict, an etheromaniac, that he smoked opium…what do I know? I didn't know, at any rate, what his vices were. When he asked me for the first time if I thought I might be his wife one day, he was thirty-two or thirty-three years old; I had barely attained my sixteenth year. That difference of age distressed him, and he never ceased to talk to me about it, imploring me not to eternalize our engagement, because he sensed that he was growing old with a deplorable rapidity. I pointed out to him in vain that the distance of age that separated us would always remain the same. 'Yes, but in a few years, I'll be an old man.'"

She paused, as if to plunge deeper into her crushing memories, and then continued:

"About a month before his disappearance he spoke to me for the first time about a distant voyage that he intended to make, and which would probably involve a very long absence, so long that he could not anticipate its term. Some time after that he asked me, abruptly, a strange question: 'If I disappeared for a few years, would you remain faithful to my memory?'

I made this exact reply: 'I'm engaged to you, and your relatives are my benefactors; as long as you are alive and you have not released me from my oath, I do not believe that I have the right to dispose of myself.'

"He embraced me chastely, like brother, as he usually embraced me, but for a little longer, and I perceived that he had been weeping. Then, before quitting me, he said: 'Swear to me that you will keep the solemn engagement that you have just made, that you will remain faithful to my memory for as long as you do not have the absolute certainty of my death.' And I swore."

Gilberte stopped again, in order to give her voice time to become firm again, and I took advantage of that to squeeze passionately the hand that she abandoned to me, for I was as distressed as she was.

"The following day," she went on, "he disappeared and we never saw him again. He had left a few ambiguous lines for his parents, a letter to his brother in which he asked him to substitute for him in the management of his affairs, even if he had to remain absent for some years, and for me, the simple words: *I am counting on your fidelity.*

"Nearly five years have passed since then, during which the image of the disappeared has never ceased to dominate my thoughts. In spite of everything, by reason of the mystery that weighed over his absence, he had left a dolorous void in my heart, a void that I did not think of filling in. I believed him to be voluntarily dead. and I reproached my lukewarm attitude toward him as if it had been the cause of his suicide, and that torturing idea drew a definitive crepe over my future as a woman. I ended up thinking that Antonio had wanted it thus, by virtue of a sort of post-mortem jealousy: having not deigned to be his wife, I ought not to be anyone's.

"We have lived very retired lives since then, in America as well as France, the last two years in Candia. Monsieur and Madame Banchi cannot console themselves for the loss of their nephew. In their eyes, moreover, I was still his fiancée, and the idea of seeking another establishment for me never occurred to them. It didn't even occur to them when, regenerated by labor and entered into grace again, Giuseppe, who had replaced his brother admirably, adopted the habit, in spring and autumn, of coming to spend a few weeks with us."

I was about to risk a timid interruption, but Gilberte was already weighing the adorable frankness of her gaze upon me.

"I can anticipate your thinking," she said. "Giuseppe has never said a single amorous word to me; he is for me an amiable comrade, attentive, even devoted, and that's all. So I've informed him of your step, begging him to keep the secret provisionally on that point as on all the rest, and I will add that he greeted the news without surprise or emotion. In any case, he is never emotional, by virtue of which his judgment is always sound and his attitude, in the most difficult circumstances of life, impregnated with the fine cold audacity that triumphs over all obstacles.

"It is for that reason that I confided in him alone the secret of the grave discovery that I made about six months ago, a discovery after which I put everything to work in order to determine my adoptive parents to come to install themselves for some time in Spalatrina.

"This is it. I sometimes had occasion to examine the secret drawers of a small items of Japanese furniture once placed in evidence on Antonio's desk, which I had taken into our new residence in Candia. The hope of finding some clue relative to the mystery of his disappearance had given me a taste for such research, and the item itself, so ingenuous in appearance—a simple hardwood box incrusted with microscopic gems—but so complicated in the interior, ended up exerting an inexplicable attraction upon me, and I came to dismantle it frequently as a mere pastime, but always with a sort of superstitious dread.

One day, having succeeded in dismantling it and opening all the compartments—all empty—of the little box, I noticed that the base, which I had believed until then to be solid wood, might have a double bottom. I was not mistaken, for after long tactile exploration, the pressure of my index finger on an almost invisible node caused an internal mechanism to operate and the double bottom opened. I found half a dozen letters on India paper, dated from Spalatrina and signed by the name Harward, but the text of which was encrypted, and also very long. The date of the last of the letters attributed it to a fortnight before Antonio's disappearance, and—a particularly significant detail—it bore on the reverse side of the final page some brief notes in Antonio's handwriting concerning the timetables of the trains and steamships to take from Louisville, where we were then resident, to Spalatrina.

"Thus, it was in Spalatrina that it was necessary to search for the key to the somber enigma, and at least the initial data susceptible of allowing the trail of the disappeared to be picked up. I was then in regular correspondence with young Suzanne Saint-Marceau, whose acquaintance I had made in Nice the previous winter, and who announced to me her departure for the famous Syrian station. While waiting for her to be able to inform me, I sought, but without success, to decipher the cryptographic text of the letters."

"I beg your pardon for interrupting you, Mademoiselle," I said. "This time, your lack of success doesn't surprise me; certain combinations resist all attempts at deciphering, and in reality, it requires long practice to arrive at translating into clear even the simplest encrypted texts."

"That was also Giuseppe's opinion, to whom I showed one of the letters, but only informing him of the discovery of the others, limiting myself to telling him that I had good reasons for supposing that they had been addressed to Antonio. He kept it for a few hours and returned it to me, confessing that he did not feel capable of deciphering such hieroglyphs."

"Perhaps," I hazarded, "by addressing yourself to a specialist..."

"That was my intention, but I could not put it into execution, because a few days later the box disappeared, with all the letters that it contained. A strange *coup de théâtre*, isn't it? But what is even stranger is that the mysterious thief of the box was a woman.

"You found it again, then?"

"No, certainly not, but when I was certain that it had not been stolen by ordinary means—no one had gone into my room except Giuseppe, who had come to bid me adieu two days before as he was about to depart for America—after reflecting hard, I examined attentively the frame of the window of my room that overlooked the garden on the ground floor. On the outside, the wall between two windows bore traces of scratches; someone had climbed up to the window and it was by that criminal means that someone had penetrated into my room.

"At the foot of the wall, the ground, all humus, bore the very clear imprint of the soles of a pair of woman's ankle-boots: disconcerting clues, in sum, but which sufficed to demonstrate that the theft must have been committed by a person unknown to me, and *by order*. Now, only two men could have had an interest in recovering that correspondence: the person to whom it was addressed, Antonio, and the one who was its author, Harward. Admitting that it was the former, that would at least have proved his existence, but any trail was lacking in that direction, and I was obliged to return to that of Harward, who appeared to reside in Spalatrina in a permanent fashion.

"One of my friends in Chicago had sojourned for some time in the majority of the ports of call in the Levant. I wrote to him at hazard, and it turned out that I was lucky, because he had resided in Spalatrina for a few months, and Harward was not unknown to him.

"Professor Harward, he told me, in substance, is one of our most distinguished compatriots, a former professor of physics at the University of Philadelphia, also a distinguished chemist, who has succeeded in syntheses reputed to be unrealizable—in brief, a kind of American Berthelot. Only his philosophical doctrines had caused difficulties for him in university milieux. He had ended up denying death, or at least claimed to have demonstrated the inanity of the cortege of terror with which it is surrounded in the human imagination. Furthermore, he claimed that a means would be found sooner or later to combat it, and to postpone its settlement for as long as possible. He was on the track himself of a great discovery of a nature to delay senility indefinitely, if not to suppress it entirely.

"In the meantime he had founded in Chicago the famous suicide club that caused so much talk,[9] and perhaps it was only necessary to see it merely as a kind of scholarly relaxation, a macabre pastime whose real purpose was to group together under the same banner all those who had a scorn for death and felt disposed to the worst sacrifices to aid in the discovery of a means to stand up to it.

"At any rate, Professor Harward fell into disgrace in elevated universitarian circles. A few of his friends in the club then told him about Spalatrina, the free city par excellence, where they had sought an atmosphere propitious for their more or less admitted insanities.. He therefore went to Spalatrina, and with the capital put at his disposal by a handful of admirers, he had founded, it was said, in the hinterland, in an almost inaccessible region, a vast private Institute sheltering the mysterious laboratories where, alone henceforth, he intended to pursue the means of confronting annihilation, of abstracting humans from the thousand causes of decay that led to death.

---

[9] The author probably has in mind the notorious Whitechapel Club of Chicago, also known as the Suicide Club, founded in 1889 by a group of newspapermen, which was disbanded in 1894. However, the only club that seems to play a role in the story is the aforementioned Club of Undesirables.

"Such was the information furnished to me by my American friend: information in consequence of which I put everything to work, as soon as winter came, to persuade my adoptive parents to make the voyage to which I owe making your acquaintance."

I bowed in response to those last words, so amiable, and took advantage of a pause on the part of the young woman to speak in my turn.

"I believe, Mademoiselle, that I can now divine he thought that has guided you: you suppose that Antonio had made the acquaintance of Professor Harward in America and that, and, as an admirer of his doctrines like so many others, he decided to make a personal sacrifice, in a measure that we do not know as yet, in order to aid the man's experiments, of a more or less dangerous nature, and that the voluminous encrypted correspondence discovered by you was a flagrant proof the trouble taken by Harward to convince his subject.

"In any case, I can understand now why someone stole that correspondence, which, in spite of its encrypted character, would have delivered the key to the affair to you sooner or later. It only remains to know whether it's Harward that has stolen it, or whether..."

"Whether it's Antonio, you mean, for you've been seized by the same suspicions as me, and you're saying to yourself: 'Antonio who, since his disappearance, had probably retired to Spalatrina, must have suffered, voluntarily or not, the same fate as Lord Cattledown.' And you'll be fortified even more in that conjecture when you know that the physician who has been caring for Cattledown in recent days is none other than Harward himself."

"However," I objected, "I thought that the mountainous hinterland where Harward was settled was inaccessible over land."

"For us, yes, because it's necessary to go around the rocky massif and undertake a perilous journey across the desert, but you're forgetting the aerial route and the hydroplane that is bobbing so coquettishly in the depths of the harbor. I found out yesterday that that hydroplane belongs to Harward."

"Good; everything is clarified, and the investigation required no longer seems to me to present any difficulty.

"If only!" said Gilberte, whose pure forehead was furrowed by an anxious crease. "Giuseppe isn't of the same opinion as you. I've told you that it was only on my insistence that he consented to accompany us to Spalatrina. He didn't know anything, absolutely nothing. But as soon as the first step I made to follow the route that was offered I understood that the task was too rude for a weak young woman, and I took him as a confidant. Certainly, he's as determined as I am to move heaven and earth to recover Antonio, dead or alive, but he preaches prudence.

"According to him, to penetrate into Harward's establishment, as is my intention, in order to do so other than by cunning or surprise, we would run into insurmountable obstacles, for our family links with the person we believe to be sequestered there, voluntarily or not, would immediately render us suspect to Harward, who would find a thousand ways to stop us.

"Yesterday evening I made him party to the step taken in your name by Madame Saint-Marceau. He congratulated me sincerely, even with a joyful emotion, be it said to reassure you if you had the slightest doubt about his sentiments in my regard."

Oh, the delicate smile feathering the slender dart with which she demolished the obscure jealousy that her woman's intuition had detected in some of my circumlocutions!

"Immediately," she went on, "He understood, like me, that you would be a precious auxiliary for us. In brief, when shaken by the well-founded objection that he opposed to my project of an expedition into the hinterland, I proposed the idea of having Lord Cattledown questioned adroitly, for want of Harward, who departed again yesterday. He approved fully. He even put you forward, saying: "That's exactly where Monsieur d'Autremont might be very useful to us, for no one suspects him of being attached to us.""

"I can only repeat to you, Mademoiselle," I said, fierily, "that I belong to you body and soul, and that from now on you can dispose of me as if..."

"Don't finish," she said, with a melancholy smile. "So many proofs await us that it's perhaps better not to alarm destiny by giving to our wishes, which are the same, too precise an expression. All that I can tell you is that I share your sentiments. I also divine in you a soul so similar to mine that it seems to me that I've always known you and always preferred you. So it's a proud joy for me to have been distinguished by you, and it would be an even greater joy to make your happiness, if the gods permit it."

She had put her hand in mine, and as I leaned toward her, she tried to extend her forehead to me, which emotion painted pale pink.

I placed my lips thereon, and it was like a chaste and secret symbol of our betrothal. Then, upset to the point of tears, I said: "However...what if we recover Antonio?"

She reflected momentarily, and then said, in a slow and grave voice: "I suppose that after five years of separation, he will have renounced me of his own accord, or, if not…I shall make him understand that his long absence has created the irreparable."

I certainly could not demand more, and we returned to talking about the projected investigation, and the fashion in which I would proceed with Lord Cattledown. It was agreed that I would present myself at his home as a writer, on the part of Saint-Marceau, and ask him, as an entry into the matter, for a few biographical details about Professor Harward, of whom I would claim to be one of his most fervent admirers. For the rest, I would draw inspiration from the circumstances.

"And now," said Gilberte, "introduce me to your dog…I'm eager to become his friend."

"He will be very happy to hear that from your lips."

I rang for my Sudanese, and an instant later, Flax irrupted into the room. I invited him to present his respects to "Mademoiselle Gilberte," but, either because he did not understand, or because he was intimidated by the beautiful foreigner and the odorous cloud that surrounded her—for the nose of a dog, at least—he advanced toward her awkwardly and unnaturally, sniffed the hem of her dress with respectful precautions, and then suddenly, thinking to find an assent in my voice that would reassure him, he stood up, placing his two front paws on the young woman's shoulders.

"Oh, what beautiful ardent and soft eyes!" exclaimed Gilberte.

And as she leaned forward, Flax darted his long pink tongue and three times, he licked the black clusters on the forehead at the same place where I had brushed it with my first kiss.

The ice was broken. Flax then sat on his backside and with his soft voice—a voice that he reserves for his intimates, for his ordinary vocal timbre is rather hoarse and cavernous—he made his new friend a long speech, stammered and hiccupped from the edges of his tremulous chops, his laughing teeth and his entire body, where ill-contained impatience and supplication were quivering.

"But what does he mean?" repeated Gilberte amazed.

"He's fêting you and complimenting you, evidently, and is in despair at the idea that you might not understand."

"But yes…but yes..."

The delicate little hand leaned gently on the silky fur of the forehead, and Flax was then appeased.

"What a pity," sighed Gilberte, "it is that we don't understand the language of dogs more clearly."

The prearranged telephone call summoned Giuseppe, who came in smiling, welcomed Gilberte's confidences, and then shook my hand warmly. He was so emotional that Italian inflexion pierced his Franco-American accent.

"I'm truly delighted to be able to consider you from now on as a member of the family."

"Let's not anticipate," said Gilberte, blushing. "It remains for us to obtain the consent of Monsieur and Madame Banchi."

"Basta! You'll have it tomorrow."

Flax's attitude was bizarre. Invariably passionate for newcomers, for better or worse, reserving for them, in accordance with their sex, the conditions and his humor of the moment, respectful accolades, cheerful curtsies or, on the contrary, a flood of terrifying invectives howled at the top of his voice, now he withdrew under a chiffonier that was his favorite place; his yellow eyes darkened and lit up by turns, obstinately aimed at Giuseppe, and he muttered incomprehensible things. It was only on my formal order that he abandoned a slack and condescending paw to the young man.

We separated, not without Giuseppe having approved vigorously of the decision made by Gilberte to send me to interview Lord Cattledown the following day.

VIII

The next day's sky displays the implacable sun of every day. I experience the lassitude of thinking that it will shine like that until the end of eternity, and that it will continue to shine until the end of everything. Fine weather that is too durable and too uniform also has its melancholy.

The house in which Lord Cattledown lives, situated on the flank of the hill, like all the respectable ones here, is an adulterous product of Gothic and Arabian architectures, which is to say that it is reminiscent of both a heavy Berlin palace and a little pocket Alhambra.

I ring at the exterior door, ogival in form, decorated with Koranic nails and a ritual hand.

A black face, old and distressed, all the wrinkles of which are definitively broken, appears at the door.

"Lord Cattledown?"

"But Monsieur the gentleman doesn't know, then..."

"No..."

"Milord is dead...last night...murdered!"

"Murdered!"

The lugubrious, tragic word rings false in the living splendor of the ambience. How can there be assassins under that sky of peace and adoration, and why has that man, whose name I did not even know a few days before, perished by violence at the precise moment when he acquired a culminating interest in my life?

I did not have time to question the negro, for the law arrived at that moment: three messieurs in the suits of well-off tourists and a fourth in a frock-coat with a red sash, the last vaguely representing the authority of the commander of believers in that tiny peninsula assimilated to private property, while the others incarnated the local—which is to say Anglo-Franco-American—judiciary and criminal police: a consul, a commissaire and a medical examiner.

As I mentioned the names of my friends Gil d'Ax and Saint-Marceau, those gentlemen invited me politely to penetrate into the house of the crime with them.

They began by interrogating the domestic staff recruited at hazard when the furnished house was rented, which consisted of an old negro porter-majordomo and a cook, seconded by two boys charged with inferior work and errands; finally, an English nurse, a deaconess of one of the numerous schismatic protestant sects scattered in Syria, cared for the aged lord, who had been very poorly since his abrupt reappearance in Spalatrina.

The account furnished by the latter, who had kept vigil over the invalid for a part of the night, ought to have taken priority over all the others. Unfortunately, it was so confused on first examination, so implausible, and discordant with the rather precise testimony of the two boys that it appeared initially to be a fable invented by the deaconess to spare her a painful confession, having yielded to sleep instead of acquitting the various functions of her ministry.

She deposed as follows:

"It might have been about four o'clock in the morning, and I was half-asleep, seeing that the lord was sleeping quite calmly, when a slight sound made me raise my head. I was sitting at the foot of the bed, my face turned toward the terrace, faintly illuminated by a crescent moon, to which the two French windows of the room were wide open as usual.

"Having raised my eyes I saw against the balusters a feminine form draped in a sort of gauze or white muslin haïk, a flap of which was drawn over her face."

"To hide her features from you, apparently," the commissaire interjected, idly.

"Yes, but all the same, I observed that she had a very pale face with ardent dark eyes. She approached the threshold of the room, moving like a phantom, so well that I was suffocating, nailed to my armchair by fear. The apparition took advantage of that to enter, gliding; at any rate, I didn't hear the slightest sound of footsteps. She approached the bed where the poor lord was still asleep, leaned over his face, and it appeared to me that she kissed him for a long time; then she straightened up and drew away silently, as she had come. When, having recovered from my fear, I leaned over the poor lord in my turn, astonished that he had not been woken up by what had just happened, him being such a light sleeper, I observed with horror that he was no longer breathing, and I perceived then that he must have received a puncture in the heart, his chemise presenting, at the height of the left breast, the trace of an almost imperceptible incision, a tiny damp red patch."

"Blood!" emphasized the intemperately precise mind of the magistrate.

It was the turn of the two boys to say what they had seen, for they claimed to have been taking the evening air under a hornbeam hedge juxtaposed with an English garden overlooked by the terrace in question.

At the time when the crime was committed they had seen a man in a burnoose enter the garden by a small service door. He was bare-headed and resembled a indigene. As he had entered tranquilly by the door, the boys assumed that he had a key to it and that he was a relative or friend of the porter; but when they saw him climb on to the terrace, aiding himself with the branches of an old fig-tree half-enclosed by the wall and then deliberately enter the lord's room, they supposed—O blasphemy!—that the nocturnal visitor was a friend of the night nurse, a friend that she could only receive clandestinely and in places where it as easy to slip away in case of surprise. Otherwise, they argued, would she not have raised the alarm?

The impious and impudent hypothesis of the two boys caused the deaconess to faint; the magistrate took advantage of that to suspend the integration, and we all went to examine the lord's room, into which, rightly, no one had penetrated since the discovery of the crime, except for a local physician summoned in haste by the porter.

The latter, who was sitting beside the bed, got up when we approached and, asked to give his advice, expressed himself in very scientific language, which I shall translate approximately.

"The death, in my opinion was occasioned by the stopping of the heart due to a lesion of that organ, a lesion followed by an internal hemorrhage, which seems to have been provoked by a profound puncture, of which you can see the trace here, at the level of the left breast. The instrument of the crime appears to have been a steel needle. But now, Messieurs, this was what struck me more in the course of an initial examination of the victim..."

With those words, he lifted up the lack handkerchief that covered the dead man's face; it was that of a man about fifty years old, entirely clean-shaven, very thin, with prominent cheek-bones, dark patches under the eyes, the mouth retracted, almost lipless, the ears diaphanous. And what was strange about the face was that the livid, bloodless skin seemed, when looked at closely, to be covered with a very fine pigmented pellicle of an indefinable color, drawn over the pale violet.

"The entire body," the physician pronounced, gravely, "presents the same phenomenon. Well, Messieurs, that skin is the skin of a man who must have been immersed entirely, and for an incalculable duration, in a liquid at a very low temperature. Now, Lord Cattledown was really alive, was he not, Messieurs?"

"Yes, certainly," replied the commissaire, coldly. "He was perfectly alive until the moment of his death."

"It's a matter, then, of a disconcerting and utterly inexplicable phenomenon."

The commissaire shrugged his shoulders. "Let's not seek to explain it, then. We're here to investigate the causes of the crime and the probable traces left by the murderer, and I can't admit any deviation from the investigation. Furthermore," he added, in a humorless fashion, "the dead man had that coloration of the face while he was alive, and no one, to my knowledge, was astonished by it or took exception to it."

The response could have been made that Lord Cattledown, having reappeared mysteriously in Spalatrina after several years of absence, had only arrived a few days ago, to shut himself away in that house, and had probably not been seen by any of his old friends, but, the English consul having agreed with the representative of the Turkish police, the incident was closed and they proceeded with the examination of the location.

Its first results were in conformity with the nurse's story; it really was a woman who had scaled the terrace, for the clear footprints left by the assassin in the humus of the flower-bed at the foot of the terrace showed the form of feminine shoes with delicate soles and high heels, curved in the so-called Louis XV style.

Furthermore, they collected from the branches of the fig-tree a few strands of the haïk in which the woman was enveloped. The commissaire then observed that the shoe-prints commenced and ended at the little door to the garden, from which he concluded that the woman must have arrived and departed in a carriage or on horseback, although the road offered no trace of wheels or hooves, but, on the contrary, several traces of masculine shoes, which appeared to him to be negligible.

Finally, it was evident that the little door to the garden had not been forced or fractured, but simply opened with a key adapted to the lock—with the consequence that the two boys appeared to have told the truth, in a certain measure, and the deaconess too. The other two domestics had not seen anything, and it only remained to conclude that initial enquiry.

Nevertheless, in order that the legal authorities did not seem to be returning empty-handed, the consul and the commissaire, having consulted briefly, decided to have the two boys locked up, their quality of indigenes having rendered them suspect.

IX

The mysterious assassination of Lord Cattledown has caused a great uproar in Spalatrina, where everyone appears to have forgotten that one can die a violent death, and that the first crime had appeared on earth with the first man, or at least with the second.

Furthermore, public opinion has adopted the version of the investigators: it is a matter of a woman. It is generally supposed that if Lord Cattledown reappeared so unexpectedly and so mysteriously in Spalatrina in order to go to ground in a private house, from which he did not emerge again after the day he entered, it is because he was fleeing a feminine vengeance, which was able to attain him regardless.

When I arrived at the Banchis' house, the bearer of the sinister news, I was received with open arms by the old couple. They knew everything, everything regarding Gilberte and me, save for the agreement made between us on the subject of the search for Antonio, of which we wanted to spare them the emotions and perhaps the dolorous surprises. It was Giuseppe who had betrayed us—for good reasons, naturally.

"You were at risk of compromising yourself," he explained to Gilberte, "so I took it upon myself to sound out my uncle and aunt adroitly, and when I saw that they were very favorably disposed toward Monsieur d'Autremont, I let it out…with a thousand oratory precautions."

In brief, Monsieur and Madame Banchi know now that I love Gilberte, and that she has promised to be my wife—and they have accepted that eventuality—as soon as the mystery of Antonio's disappearance in completely elucidated, in respect of which we are supposed to be relying on the active efforts of Giuseppe.

The latter has become all the dearer to them because the marriage in question threatens them with a curt abandonment, so the aged Banchis have given me to understand that they are transferring to him all the successive prerogatives with which they had invested Antonio—a delicate means of informing me that Gilberte's dowry will be modest. Giuseppe cannot abandon half the heritage to Gilberte, as Antonio would have done, to constitute a dowry for the latter, who would have become his wife. That is only logical, and Giuseppe will learn himself, at the first opportunity, that Gilberte and I will not accept anything from his hand. I'm sufficiently rich for two.

In any case, she and I have many other things that preoccupy us at present.

"Do you know," she said to me a moment ago, "what strikes me the most about the lugubrious adventure in which poor Lord Cattledown disappeared?"

And she specified, emphasizing each word: "It's a woman who stole Professor Harward's correspondence at the moment when, having fallen into my hands, it might have delivered the secret of Antonio's disappearance to me, and it's a woman again who has murdered Lord Cattledown at the moment when we were founding on him a hope attached to the same order of ideas."

This time, the connection is so precise and so obvious that I feel gripped by an inexpressible anguish. Someone, therefore, is spying on Gilberte, divining her intimate thoughts, ready for anything—yes, even crime—to prevent her from obtaining the goal she has set herself.

And who can tell, in that case, whether Gilberte's own life might be threatened?

But how, in the other hand, can such a fantastic hypothesis be admitted? Only Giuseppe and I, thus far, are informed of her projects. Now, Giuseppe is above suspicion, and in any case, it's a matter of a woman and not a man.

Certainly, the two boys claim to have seen a man and not a woman, but their affirmations on that point are reduced to negligibility by the imprints found in the garden and on the terrace itself.

I adopt a tone as indifferent as possible in order not to alarm the beloved more than is necessary.

"Do you suspect someone in your entourage, my ear Gilberte?"

"Absolutely no one. Besides which, here in Spalatrina the question can't even be posed. We scarcely receive anyone and no one or almost no one knows us; I have no other friend than Suzanne Saint-Marceau and I haven't confided our secret to anyone, not even to her."

"Might Giuseppe have committed some indiscretion?"

"He has given me his word of honor that he has not told a living soul about our projects, and I have no reason not to believe him, for he has never lied, and finally, he has no connections in Spalatrina, any more than I have. Furthermore, he has only told his uncle and aunt what he could without betraying our common secret, and they still don't know the story of the discovery of the encrypted letters and the veritable reason for our sojourn in Spalatrina."

"The mystery seems impenetrable, then."

A great sadness descends upon me. Gilberte has abandoned her little slender white hand to me, and that tiny part of her, of her living sweetly-perfumed flesh, puts us in sufficient communion for me to perceive the accelerated rhythm of her heart.

I don't know what dress she has on, nor what jewelry she is wearing; I can't make here the classic description of a couturier or bluestocking socialite that would be necessary. I'm not one of those who remark most of all, in a beloved woman, the details that are not her; perhaps they influence me without my being aware of it, but I don't see them; I only see the face, and the soul that illuminates that face, the curve of the forehead, the fleeting reflection of the eyes, and the bow of the lips, which constitute the psychic effigy of a person. In Gilberte, all of that is tragic, and what saddens me is that I don't have the right or the power to exorcize in her that element of mourning, having chosen her among all precisely because she showed that fatal sign unwittingly.

No, I don't have the right to complain if my beautiful dream is darkened by a veil of crepe, or illuminated by the repugnant vermilion of murder, but what I do lament, and which consternates me and exasperates me utterly, is the unreality in which I'm floundering, the disconcerting implausibility of the coincidences over which we stumble at every step forward, these people who disappear and reappear without anyone knowing why or how, the phantom woman who steals correspondence and murders lords at the precise moment that it thwarts our secret plans so terribly, all the way to the marbled, imbricated skin of the murdered lord, skin whose aquarium tint confounds the men of the Faculty and would, in fact, defy the pen of as Baudelaire.

I think about a unique friend that I have in Paris, who knows me well, and who advised me to leave as soon as possible precisely because he knows me well.

"You'll come back to us cured, damn it! And that's worth a few days of sea-sickness aboard Gil d'Ax's boat." Today, if he were up to date with events, I can hear him say, thunderous and ribald, as always: "Damn it…who, then, is the swine who amuses himself weaving such ludicrous plots?"

And he would be right, for it has an air of madness, the imbroglio in which we're struggling, the air of a wager, or the tale of a morphinomaniac, and is, in reality, a sinister pond stagnating outside the magical castle of my amour, a morass of spells in which I don't want us to be bogged down too long, for the ditch gives off a confused odor of blood, a singular emanation of biochemical corruption.

Because I want to clarify the matter, I've decided to resume the investigation of the murder on my own account. I'm proceeding with a sage slowness, infinite precautions, and a mania for importunate discourse on which I've prided myself, as a virtue, since childhood.

And the charming Gilberte has scolded me in vain, and tried all diabolical seductions on me in order to persuade me to put a double cork in it; I'm taking my time, sounding the terrain, trying to take the mystery from behind, advancing like a creeping Comanche on the warpath.

I've spent three days setting up, at the central crossroads of my enquiry, the following syllogism, the meditation of which Gilberte proposed to me before I set forth. We have no chance of determining the motive for the murder of the lord, unless we interrogate someone who knew him more or less intimately. Now, only one man in Spalatrina seems to have know him intimately enough, since he seems to have cared for him recently, and we even suspect him of having played a role in the lord's mysterious reappearance: Professor Harward.

So, it's necessary to interrogate, or have someone else interrogate, Professor Harward—with regard to whom, besides, Giuseppe has emitted this strange suspicion: "Who can tell whether, in spite of all appearances and the traces of the Louis XV footwear, he isn't the murderer?"

Giuseppe affirms, on the other hand—and he's evidently right—that our situation with regard to Harward hasn't changed: we ought not to reveal ourselves, ought not to make any personal approach to him. We were counting on the revelations of Lord Cattledown; he has disappeared, but the law is standing over his cadaver, and it is the law henceforth, however little it can be pushed—and Giuseppe is promising to push it—who can hold Harward to account. We have only to fold our arms, therefore, and await his deposition.

X

In fact, the law, influenced by rumors cleverly stoked up by Giuseppe, has sent an invitation to Professor Harward asking him to come in order to furnish some information verbally regarding his relationship with Lord Cattledown, information that might facilitate the investigation of the crime and the search for the criminal.

"But how can that summons reach Harward, since the mountainous massif on which his Institute is perched is inaccessible from here?"

"It's quite simple," Giuseppe replies, who, it appears, has obtained information from a good source this morning. "The massif does in fact, radiate toward Spalatrina a series of ridges that are quite impracticable, and elsewhere, it encloses the entire bay with sheer cliffs. But we, the newly disembarked, don't know that although it's situated in Syria, Spalatrina is linked to the nearest Egyptian port, Kaba, by wireless telegraph, and Harward, for his part, has equipped his Institute with a radiotelegraphic station, which permits communication with Kaba.

"Agree that it would be extraordinary, in any case, if such an important establishment were to remain isolated from the civilized world, without any other communication than the precarious road that goes directly from Kaba to Harward's Institute through twenty leagues of desert."

"That road, in any case, doesn't appear on any map."

"In fact, a part of it, the one that leads to the establishment through the mountain gorges, has been constructed at great expense by Harward himself, and the other, that of the desert, is confounded, I believe, with the old caravan route between Egypt and Syria."

"All right—but how will Harward, according to you, respond to the summons?"

"He has a choice of two ways, that of the air, by hydroplane, or the desert route—a day and a half on horseback—and the little coastal steamer that makes the journey from Kaba to Spalatrina in ten hours."

"But the coater only makes the journey every ten days."

"Indeed, so he'll probably choose the aerial route as he has done recently. There's only one hydroplane in the bay now, whereas there were two when we arrived. Both belonged to the engineer Diamantopoulos, who ceded one of them—a two-seater—to Harward last year. Perhaps it's that one that served to transport Lord Cattledown from the Institute, where he was being treated, to the house that had been rented for him here; it is, in any case, by the aerial route that Harward responded last week to the appeal of his patient, who was requesting his care, and it was also by the aerial route that he must have departed, since the two-seater hydroplane is no longer in the bay. We can conclude that it's by the aerial route that he'll return."

"Bravo, Giuseppe," said Gilberte, smiling. "You're the most precious and the most rapid of informants, and doubtless you'd have made an admirable detective. My opinion at present is that Monsieur d'Autremont should take advantage of the official presence of the professor in Spalatrina to try to meet him under some pretext and interview him adroitly."

Giuseppe's face darkened. "I doubt that he'll agree to a meeting, for Harward only receives people strongly recommended, and even the false pretext of a illness wouldn't work in this case, because he claims only to practice medicine in favor of his personal friends. Nevertheless, Monsieur d'Autremont can try, while acting in a fashion that won't compromise the success of our ulterior enterprises."

I can't explain Giuseppe's fears very well and I attribute them to an excess of suspicion relative to Harward. So, I've decided to follow my idea, no matter what the cost, as soon as the arrival of the celebrated professor is announced...

A rumor has just burst forth underneath us, in the florid square that the terrace, parallel to the strand, overhangs slightly, suspended over the waves that splash beneath in a veritable tropical garden. The large luxury automobiles that are seen passing at all hours of the day at high speed over the delightful promenade are immobilized, and the pedestrians too. All heads are orientated toward the shore, noses in the air.

"Look," says Giuseppe. "There he is."

And there is the habitual optical illusion: a black dot growing in the bosom of a cloud; soon it is an albatross, wings deployed, allowing itself to veer toward the coast; finally, the hieratic human head—a simple dot on an I, but which incarnates all strength—is silhouetted in the center of the wings.

The impression is complex, variable in accordance with imaginations; some think of the danger and sense themselves balanced between aguish and respectful admiration; others, reckless fantasists, imagine a god sitting in the middle of an empty trough. All of them, however, will applaud at the moment when the pilot will settle gently on the waves of the harbor, against the piles of the pier.

I have seized the binoculars that Gilberte holds out to me and I try to discern the features of the man who occupies, unknown to him, such an important place in my life. It's difficult, the peaked visor of a considerable helmet surpasses the nose by half a inch, and the mouth, virtually the only visible feature, is so voluble that it no longer has any expression. Harward is conversing with someone who has advanced for a handshake and is shaking the hand extended toward the aviator energetically.

"Gil d'Ax!"

That cry of joyful surprise informs my friends about the possibilities designed by my binoculars. In any case, I say to them immediately:

"This is a precious opportunity; since Gil d'Ax is so familiar with Harward, he can introduce me to him. Excuse me; I'll hop down to the beach and come back."

"Be prudent!" intimates the index finger placed over the lips of Giuseppe, who is decidedly tremulous.

A disappointment awaits me down below. Harward has just departed for the Palais de Justice; it's Gil d'Ax who tells me that, after the requisite accolade.

"I thought you were in Jaffa!" I said to him

"I went there but I didn't linger. History is an eternal recommencement; there's plague down there, and as I value my old skin, wrinkled and tanned as it might be..."

"Admitted. I didn't know that you knew the man of the day here, the one whose hand you've just shaken."

"Me neither, for the good reason that I didn't know that he'd emigrated to the Syrian coast. I made his acquaintance at the Chicago Exposition,[10] where he presented some astonishing applications of liquid air. You know that Harward is a man of great value, something like a Berthelot combined with a Roux or a Metchnikoff."

"In America he's less appreciated, for I'm weary of hearing it said that the boldness of his scientific experiments and his psychic doctrines have put him in such bad odor with public opinion that he's been obliged to exercise his genius in other latitudes."

"No one is a prophet in his own country. Look, here he is coming back. I'll introduce you, under what title?"

I'm slightly embarrassed; Gil d'Ax knows nothing about my engagement, and it's agreed between us that the Banchis' name will never be pronounced; however, I have a horror of duplicity and my friend is one of those frank and honest individuals whom one is reluctant to deceive.

Harward is already upon us, and spares me an immediate response. We salute one another. Turning to Gil d'Ax, he says: "The deputy, in conference for half an hour, has asked me to be patient, so I've come to cast a glance over my engine, which was rattling slightly just now. It's very curious, the effect of marine damp—which is to say, the vapor of sea water—on the carburetion of the benzene that I used here..."

With that, a concise theory that the chemist seemed to be explaining to us by turns, is scrupulously shared between us, with a small supplementation of gestures

---

[10] It is unclear whether this refers to the Chicago exposition of 1893 or that of 1903, but in either case it implies a setting for the story prior to the Great War.

addressed to me, the courteous attention that one owes to a new acquaintance.

Gil d'Ax allows him to speak, deferentially, and then, at the first bifurcation, introduces us to one another.

The scientist salutes me with a politeness and a cordiality devoid of any affectation. I don't believe that anyone in the world has, to such a high degree as him, the instinct or the gift of nuances of gesture and voice. His attire, like his speech, has a discreet elegance, irreproachable all the way to his shirt buttons, simple diamonds that have nothing exaggeratedly sumptuous about them. He wears his hair very short; his face, entirely clean-shaven, nevertheless does not appear harsh or ascetic, for the oval mask is plump rather than thin, the forehead not too high, the mouth ardent and healthy, the well-modeled nose straight and fleshy. At times the gaze has an extraordinary profundity and intensity of life— only at times, in the rare moments, when Harward is absorbed in speaking, for, ordinarily, his steel-gray eyes remain, in the calm orbit of the eyebrows, lakes of mildness and serenity.

I utter a great lie and keep watch on the lakes in question for the lapse that would be necessary to touch the bottom of them, but only a few concentric ripples play on the surface of the pupils. I have broached the desire that I had to interview him about his Institute for a magazine article.

"It's just," he said, in the most natural manner in the world, "that I truly don't know how or when I'd be able to give you the half-hour you're asking of me. It's six o'clock in the evening. My deposition will certainly last quite a long time, so that I can't even foresee the hour when I'll be dining, and as I'm obliged to leave tomorrow at dawn..."

"Perhaps there's a means of arranging everything," Gil d'Ax intervenes. "Having returned from my excursion I have the intention of devoting my evening to my numerous friends here, some of whom have already been alerted by telephone; we'll be meeting at my place—which is to say, my apartment at the Splendid Palace—at eleven, and you'd give me great pleasure if you'd like to honor me by join us."

This time, Harward has no hesitation.

"I accept gladly," he said, smiling, "and I'll have the double pleasure of stirring a few memories of Chicago and satisfying your friends curiosity.

With that, the professor resumes the road to the Palais, and I'm astonished by that simple and cordial welcome on the part of a person that Giuseppe supposed to be unapproachable, bristling with suspicion and armored by guile, cunning and maleficent duplicity.

While Gil runs back to the telephone—for he wants to honor Harward with a reception of great splendor, of which his name and presence will furnish three-quarters of the expense—I go to take the good news to Gilberte.

Giuseppe is with her. As surprised as me by the ductility—the word is Giuseppe's—of Harward, they are nevertheless delighted and congratulate me on the mastery with which I have been able to conduct the affair. Gilberte wants me to take her to that impromptu soirée, but I dissuade her; she is too pretty to pass unperceived, Gil d'Ax or his wife would be obliged to introduce her to the scientist, and once his suspicions are awakened all my efforts to make him talk will be in vain.

She yields to my reasoning and Giuseppe declares spontaneously that he is in the same situation as her. In

any case, he does not want to appear at that soirée because he has a great revenge to take on one of his
friends, too imprudently fortunate at poker the previous
evening. I can only approve of his abstention.

XI

The pavilion of the Splendid Palace where Gil d'Ax receives his guests, with its low-arched portico, its moucharabiehs and its Moorish lanterns, presents a pretty décor of the old Orient, modernized by electric light, where, around Gil d'Ax, always decked out like a corsair, and his wife, a creole "creolizing," according to him, some twenty women in simple beachwear are gathered, and a restricted number of dinner jackets, the climate excluding any minutiae of etiquette.

The women are talking all languages except French, the official language; they represent all the technical and national types of Europe, originating from all over the world—for once again I have noticed something rather curious here: the varieties of the European type contain, more or less ostentatiously, all the types of the globe, from the most obvious dolichocephalic blond to the most bestial Oceanian savage.

I have before my eyes Swedes, Russians, Danes and Frenchwomen—the last-named rare—some of whom, in the feline lines of the face, their bestial eyes umbrageous, merit being born in Malaysia or Polynesia. So it is true that we descend from a single unique stock, of which the branches, even the most evolved, still reproduce in abundance, more or less faithfully, the common ancestral type, which is perhaps that of the anthropomorphic ape.

Gil d'Ax strolls as if at home among the groups of women whose bare shoulders, where brilliants go astray in humble fifty-centime lace, spread perfumes that cause headaches. He has been able cleverly to stimulate their curiosity to white heat by telling them fantastic stories regarding Professor Harward, who is expected at any moment, like the stories that are invented nowadays in salons with the elements of mementos of pathology, popularized for the usage of socialites.

Eleven o'clock has chimed. It's the exact time when Harward ought to make his appearance, according to a note written in his own hand when he emerged from the Palais de Justice, which a Libyan messenger brought thereafter to Gil d'Ax. The scientist is, it appears, so meticulous in his punctuality that he leaves nothing to chance, even the hours of his social pleasures.

This time, however, he is in default, for now it is nearly half past midnight and he has not appeared. The ladies, who are scarcely tempted by the buffet, and getting impatient and bred; Lucette Saint-Marceau becomes their spokesperson to reproach Gil d'Ax for having tricked them.

"You know that I'm incapable of it," Gil protests, finally. "I'll go to the Libyan myself and bring Harward back."

At that moment a new missive from the scientist was brought. He read it and, perplexed, communicated its contents to us.

When you receive this word, Harward wrote, *I will have departed for the Institute again by air. Thus fate has decided. Excuse me, and be assured that only a grave and unexpected circumstance could have constrained me to break my word, and, above all, to renounce the pleasure of spending a few minutes in the company of you and yours.*

"Has Monsieur Harward really gone?" Gil d'Ax asked, having retained the bearer of the message and talking to him on one side.

"Yes, Monsieur, a good half an hour ago," stammered the latter. "He received two visits after afternoon. A beautiful demoiselle first, who wept a lot and begged him a lot. But he didn't want to know and send beautiful demoiselle packing. All right! Then he got dressed, perhaps to go see sidi. But before leaving, new visit."

"Another beautiful demoiselle?" mocked Gil d'Ax.

"No, veiled woman, long haïk, she very angry, palaver much, gesticulates. Sidi Harward very angry too. Then woman leave. Then Sidi Harward reflect, hands in head like this, and then he write this paper and gives it to me, and goes away."

Right away, I leave Gil d'Ax with his guests and I go to the club where Giuseppe had told me to pick him up after midnight. I take him away from his poker game in order to recount the events, and I don't hide it from him that I'm anxious. Might the beautiful demoiselle sent away by Harward before the arrival on the scene of the other woman have been Gilberte?"

He reassures me immediately on that point. He only left the house two hours ago and Gilberte, in a peignoir, was occupied in reading. She was extremely calm, even cheerful, and had asked him to tell me that she counted on spending part of the night in the company of Lamartine. "Furthermore," he added, "she's incapable of deceiving us."

That plural moves me agreeably, while dissipating doubts that I do not hesitate to qualify as absurd now.

They were, in fact, for, having accepted the amiable proposal to accompany Giuseppe to his house, in spite of the late hour, we find Gilberte reading on the little terrace, from the corner of which one can see the entire bay.

81

The night is warm, of a vaporous and ashy blue through which the moon is trailing her dazzling veils. Space is full of the unreal, the magical; the most immaterial dream would dissolve there, because it would only be human.

Gilberte is reading the odes of Lamartine, her favorite poet, and is herself, this evening, exactly as I once imagined the heroines of the singer of Elvire. She evokes his voyage to Syria. At least he knew the enchantments of this sky before sinking into the forgetfulness and ingratitude of his time. But what would he have said, if he had seen, like me a little while age, Professor Harward's thundering airplane passing through that sky of dreams?

That thought unleashes my commentaries, aimed this time at the unexpected apparition at the Libyan of a mysterious woman, and her altercation, which appears to have determined the professor to depart again immediately instead of keeping the promise that he had made to Gil d'Ax.

"Always the woman in the haïk," says Gilberte, in a voice that trembles slightly.

And that remark translates my own thought. Once again, it's a mysterious veiled woman who emerges at a given point to prevent Harward, apparently with the aid of threats, from rendering to an invitation useful to our cause.

"Pooh!" Giuseppe interjects, slyly. "Not extraordinary, if we consider that the brief quarrel between Harward and the woman was preceded by a short scene in which the heroine was a young European woman without any evident attachment to the former. I imagine, in the final analysis, that our Harward is simply caught up in the intrigues of a woman, with the consequence that he is more to be pitied than criticized. But we'll talk about it again tomorrow...I'll leave you lovers...each according to his lot...you to sweet dreams and me to the heavy sleep of the just—which is to say, the gambler who has finally skinned an opponent who was excessively lucky the day before."

And he does indeed disappear.

We remain for a few moments, lips sealed. I contemplate my beautiful fiancée, and a swell of distress roils in my emotional breast. Somber now, her splendid eyes have ceased to reflect the star of the sky, and it seems to me that it's my fault. Come on, it's obvious, I'm a coward. What! I love that delectable creature, I intend to make her mine and devote my entire life to her in exchange, and I stand here quibbling and procrastinating, measuring with a pale eye the obstacles that a diabolical hand is striving to accumulate between our happiness and us.

"What are we going to do now?"

I don't know which of us has posed the question, but it's evident that the time for action has come. Giuseppe will make every effort to procure us Harward's deposition concerning Lord Cattledown, in full, but what does it matter? I'm sure in advance that it won't tell us anything very interesting, that in any event, it won't inform us of what it's necessary to attempt or not to attempt in order to know whether Antonio is dead or alive—and it's necessary that we know that as soon as possible.

"Listen," I say to Gilberte, "will you permit me to talk to you with an open heart?"

The dear face becomes animated and colored, and the eyes of dream into which my eyes plunge give me the sensation of a fall into the divine ether.

"Could you talk to me otherwise?"

"That's true; in reciting clichéd words, as well as expressing what one feels most profoundly, one makes use of ready-made phrases that betray thought. Pardon me; I simply want to ask your permission to express my personal opinion on our case—which is to say, my intimate opinion, disengaged from any foreign influence, freed from any consideration of ambience.

"We're convinced, aren't we, that Antonio has resided for some time, and perhaps still resides, at Harward's Institute. Well, our duty is to go there, with rigorous precautions, to try to penetrate into it, on no matter what condition, even if we have to use deception, or to employ force. Let's understand one another, though. The journey is difficult and fatiguing, since it traverses immense uncultivated plains perhaps infested by the traditional Bedouin marauders; in brief, it's almost an expedition. I don't believe that it's a woman's place to run the risks or confront the perils, but if Giuseppe wants to accompany me, I think the two of us might succeed quite easily, once we reach the place, of penetrating the mystery that weighs so dolorously upon your destiny…and mine."

"In associating our two destinies, as you've just done, and as we want them to be in the future, you've underlined the weak point of your argument," protested Gilberte. "What! You're going to confront the perils of which you speak, you who never knew Antonio and are only obeying a generous inclination..."

"Pardon me, my dear Gilberte, "don't make me any grander, any nobler than I am; it isn't generosity that is dictating my conduct in this instance, but the absolute need to emerge from the uncertainty that this somber history weighs upon a hope that has become my sole reason for existence."

"So be it, but that hope has found, as you know, an echo in my own heart, and your sole reason for living and acting has become mine too. And since, finally, I ought to be your wife, Monsieur d'Autremont, my place, from now on, is by your side, especially in an enterprise in which, for you at least, I alone am the cause."

The woman who wants to prove to you that she loves you, always wins her cause. I was too troubled by the dear confessions implicit in all she said in or to try to struggle; however in capitulating on my personal account, I did not lose sight of other considerations, those that put her reputation on the line had to have a voice in the matter.

"What will society say?"

"Nothing at all, for young women enjoy here, as you know, an entirely American liberty. In any case, Giuseppe will be with us."

"Indeed, but I have friends here, good Frenchmen, for whom our engagement is still secret. Don't you fear…?"

She interrupted me, smiling.

"I've confided our secret to Suzanne; if you make Monsieur and Madame Saint-Marceau party to it, as well as Gil d'Ax, we'll be covered."

"I'll obey you with the greatest joy," I said, radiant at the authorization she had given me. "It will perhaps remain to convince your parents of the necessity of your joining an expedition in which your collaboration isn't indispensable."

"Believe me, I'll convince them more easily than we'll convince Giuseppe of the opportunity of the expedition itself, for he's very opposed in principle, as you know, to any direct and personal contact with Harward.

We have nothing to gain from it, he says, and everything to lose."

And as Gilberte looked at me with a suddenly anxious expression, I hastened to express a reassuring opinion regarding Giuseppe's good dispositions.

"He must have recognized since, the scant value of his preventive measures, since I've seen Harward and he consented to an interview with me. I'll see our man on my own, if necessary. He'll be flattered that I've made such a journey in order to remind him of his promise, and that will simplify everything."

Gilberte remained visibly preoccupied, but as we would be fixed the following day regarding Giuseppe's dispositions, it was pointless to discuss it any longer.

We separated, and the night seemed so beautiful— or, rather the morning, for dawn was about to sketch its Puvis de Chavannes frescoes in the east—that I renounced going to bed, only imitating in that three-quarters of the winter visitors, who inverted during the six months of their sojourn all the hours of life.

The next day, toward noon, I had myself announced again at Gilberte's house with Giuseppe, who arrived at the same time as me. He was in a frock-coat, an unbreakable plastron and a ceremonial black cravat circling the stiff collar, which one might have thought enameled, so shiny was it, even in the shadow.

Inclined, smiling, he hastened to deposit on Gilberte's knees a manuscript of several pages: the copy he had just had the clerk make of Harward's deposition in the Lord Cattledown affair. I shall transcribe the principal passages.

Q. "You knew the victim, since you gave him your cares very recently. Will you tell us how you know him?"

Professor Harward is cold, affected; he expresses himself with tight lips; at times a suspicious gleam lurks in the depths of his pupils and he does not always reply in an immediate fashion.

(That psychological note has been traced in the margin of the minute by the deputy.)

A. "I'll tell you, but I warn you that it has no connection with the crime that, for me, remains inexplicable, since no interest or passion whatsoever, to all evidence, was in play."

Q. "Light sometimes springs forth from circumstances most foreign to the drama, and some insignificant detail can determine the important discovery that will put a magistrate on the right track, so leave to the law the care of assembling, comparing and concluding."

A. "I made Lord Cattledown's acquaintance in Chicago about ten years ago, before fixing my residence in Spalatrina—which is to say, before constructing, at my own expense, the establishment in the mountains that you know."

Q. "We only know it by hearsay, but no matter; continue."

A. "Although furnished with all my diplomas, I have never exercised the profession. Pathology and therapeutics interested me, and more particularly those relevant in one way or another to biological chemistry, the domain of which extends, whatever anyone might think, to neural dynamics. Lord Cattledown was a neuropath whose vital equilibrium was beginning to be eroded by senile intoxication, vulgarly called old age.

"At the time when I founded my Institute, which is neither a sanitarium nor a clinic, as is thought, but simply a biological chemistry station equipped for my personal studies, Lord Cattledown came to Spalatrina to request the reparation of his nerves from the Syrian climate. He was not really ill, in the current sense of the word, but he was aging too rapidly—more rapidly than one ought to age in the region of sixty. His case was interesting; I consented to care for him."

(Here the deputy indicates a pause on the part of the professor, who seems to hesitate or meditate—it is unclear which—but he continues almost immediately, his voice clear and calm.)

"And he was cured, thanks to my treatment—by which I mean that I succeeded in abstracting him from the senile intoxication that menaced him, for a number of years at least double the interval that the treatment had lasted, which is an appreciable result."

Q. "What was the duration of the treatment?"

A. "Between six and seven years, but I repeat once again that all this is of no interest to anyone but me and has no connection with the crime for which you are seeking the motive and the author. Perhaps I will decide one day to publish notes on my work and my therapeutic experiments—which is to say, on the treatment and cure of old age, at least anticipated old age—but for the moment, I cannot say any more about that subject, and I request in advance permission to retrench myself behind professional secrecy in the event of being questioned regarding a few other cures that I have been able to undertake since."

Q. "We give you that permission, since the law has no interest in any such enquiry, but will you please conclude the story of the late lord's cure."

"My...biochemical treatment extends, as I have said, over several year. It offers the inconvenience of the majority of regimes that aim to delay nutrition, diminishing, not to say suspending, vital oxidation. It dishabituates from living, it substitutes a vegetative state, that of anabiosis, as we say today, which is, in principle, the antagonist of the animistic state, given that it depresses muscular strength. Which means that, today, one cannot resume normal life without shock, at the end of the treatment. It is necessary first to prime the organism again, to reeducate the organs, to render functional energy to the tissues, the viscera and the nervous system.

"When Lord Cattledown manifested he desire to return to Spalatrina—he was impatient to see that city of dream and indolence again, where he ought to find death—I showed him the dangers to which he would expose himself by not observing the necessary transitions, above all the fatigue of a voyage through the desert, with unexpected turns that are sometimes perilous. He spoke to me about having himself conveyed in a Sedan chair, and he was so enthusiastic to resume the harness of social life, so delighted no longer to feel the burden of senility on his shoulders, so eager to live—which is to say, to use his muscles and his health as before—that he would have committed any and all follies. I spared him that, at least, and one night, while he was asleep, I transported him in my airplane to the house that he had rented a month before.

"The effect of that abrupt transplantation was salutary, in the sense that it nailed him to a chaise-longue for a few weeks, like the simple convalescent he was. I believe that he understood then how right I was to exhort him to moderation, to spare himself, and only to rehabituate himself slowly to living; at any rate, when I had occasion to see him about three weeks ago—he had asked me to call on him at the first opportunity—he thanked me again very warmly for all that I had done for him and swore to me that he would conform henceforth to the diet and the rules of hygiene that constituted his treatment of convalescence.

"That concludes, Messieurs, all the information I can give you, for, unfortunately, I did not see my client alive again."

Q. "Are you of the same opinion as your colleague Dr. Start regarding the causes that led to the late lord's death?"

A. "There cannot be any doubt on that subject."

Q. "Have you an opinion regarding the motives for this incomprehensible crime?"

A. "None. I am all the more at a loss to explain it as the presence of my client in Spalatrina ought to have been unknown to everyone."

Q. "That is where you're mistaken; his mysterious reappearance among us made him the object of all conversations; the domestic doubtless talked; and I remember one rather bizarre particularity: it was claimed that he was completely ignorant of the meaning of certain new words, or of relatively recent creation, such as the word airplane—nor had he the slightest idea of the possibility of human flight. How can that rumor be reconciled with the fact that the lord had been transported here by air?

A. "In the simplest fashion in the world. My client was ignorant, in general, of all the novelties of progress or public life, as so many new creations, posterior to his entry to the Institute, since from that moment on he was living the vegetative life imposed on him by the treatment, necessarily implying isolation and abstention from all reading.

"Nevertheless, if people were not yet flying in that epoch,[11] it would be an error to believe that the word 'airplane' was unknown. For many years Professor Richet, Frenchman, had been designating by that vocable the kinds of gliding apparatus that were tried out from time to time, and writers in scientific circles were making use of the word. If the late lord knew nothing about that it is because in his somewhat frivolous society, people are not much occupied with science, and it is thus that he was able to arrive on the threshold of the seven years that were to be the last of his life without suspecting the astounding progress realized by the machine whose name he did not now. Similarly, he was unaware that he had come here by air, because it was during one of the profound bouts of somnolence to which he was prone that I decided to accomplish the voyage of which he as so ardently desirous."

Q. "Thank you, Professor."

His deposition, in fact, tells us absolutely nothing concerning the assassination of the regretted lord. If it is the same for the papers put under seal, it is to be feared that the crime will remain forever impenetrable and unpunished.

"That's absolutely my opinion," declared Giuseppe, by way of conclusion, taking his eyes off the last page of the manuscript. He had read us the text with intonations, pauses, changes of voice, almost like an actor, and with a feverish gesticulation that I would have found exces-

---

[11] Since Cattledown's treatment has lasted seven years, this implies that the story is must surely set earlier than 1910.

sive had it not been for the nervousness with which all three of us were struggling.

"So be it," said Gilberte. "Let's leave the crime, which, without being indifferent to us, doesn't solicit our interest greatly, and ought not to deflect us from the goal that we're pursuing. I find that certain passages in the professor's deposition furnish us with further support for out gravest conjectures. This patient whose treatment lasted for year, whom it was necessary to 'dishabituate from living,' restricted to regime of complete inertia, whose organs were reduced to a minimum of vegetative life in order to reeducate them slowly subsequently, re-string 'animistic' life…all that might be the case with Antonio, and would explain, in any event, his stubborn disappearance, his absolute silence for years."

"All that, unfortunately," articulated Giuseppe in a discouraged voice, "also justifies all our suspicions with regard to Harward, and makes me fear that we'll never get anything out of the man. If Antonio really has put himself in his hands in the same conditions as Lord Cattledown, Harward will invoke professional secrecy, as he has just done before official justice."

"We'll force him to speak!" I cried, suddenly carried away by an overexcitement exasperated by the mere fact that Giuseppe was representing the situation to us as more desperate.

"Yes," Gilberte approved, "For we've just decided to go in person to the Institute and to extract the truth from Harward no matter what the cost."

"A pure folly," said Giuseppe, "which I won't allow you to commit."

But Gilberte's voice was vibrant and her eyes were emitting flashes by which I was dazzled.

"Don't say that, Giuseppe, for we're counting, on the contrary, on your collaboration, and I can't see how we can do it without you."

Giuseppe raised his arms, impotently. "But I swear to you that you won't obtain anything by that violence. I believe myself to be a sufficient observer to be able to affirm that that man has an audacity that nothing can overcome." And, his gaze vague, he added in a casual tone, seemingly forgetful of the grave question at stake. "The audacity of a madman, or at last a semi-madman."

"Monsieur d'Autremont doesn't judge him thus," riposted Gilberte.

"Indeed," I said, supportively. "He gave me the impression of being a very energetic man, undoubtedly, but very correct, very lucid, and very much master of himself."

Giuseppe enveloped me with a smile of amicable indulgence.

"It's your duty to approve of all Gilberte's extravagances, to yield to all her caprices, as it's mine to oppose the arrests of prudence and cold reason. However, since you're both irreducible, for I sense that you are, I won't insist and I incline before your combined wills. I'm yours...simply remember, if this turns out badly, that I was opposed to this turn...," He underlined the words with a smile and added: "It's true that it would be a paltry consolation. Anyway, I have no desire to triumph...on the contrary, I'll study our itinerary and our means of action closely in order to reduce to a minimum the errors that lie in wait for us. Give me two or three days, and in the meantime, equip yourselves..."

On the point of leaving he turned round to make us this recommendation, proving that he had thought of everything:

"And, in fact, don't tell anyone about our true destination, even our most intimate acquaintances; there's no need to let everyone into the secret of our voyage."

Gilberte assured him that she would only account for her displacement to her adoptive parents; as for me, Gil d'Ax was about to go on a cruise and I only saw the Saint-Marceaus, to whom I apologized for a disappearance susceptible of being prolonged sufficiently to make them anxious, and which, in consequence, might be the equivalent of a lack of correction toward them.

XII

At the Saint-Marceaus' house, Gilberte and I fall upon a tearful scene that intrigues and saddens us, but Suzanne, who is bearing the sole expense of it, will soon explain its genesis.

To begin with, there is the joyful surprise of Lucette, delighted to learn that we have so quickly brought to a good conclusion the idyll knotted under her auspices. Even Suzanne, a little confused, dries her tears in order to embrace Gilberte tenderly and murmur in her ear: "You're luckier than I am."

"That reflection, in which Gilberte divined an allusion, which she did not understand, astonished and moved her sufficiently to make her closet her young friend in a neighboring room, where she immediately subjected her to a formal interrogation.

"Why, then am I luckier than you, my dear Suzanne?"

"Simply because I've been refused consent to marry as I intend."

Gilberte was amazed. "How, then, do you intend to do it?"

"Immediately, with the man I love."

"But you're scarcely eighteen, darling, so there's no urgency, and..."

"Possibly, but they want me to wait three years—which is to say, three centuries; three years, at the end of which I'll be twenty-one, almost an old spinster, and the man I've chosen will no longer want me."

95

"He's a monster and a fool, then, but it's impossible that he's your elect. Explain to me why the three years, which do, in fact, seem excessive in your case."

"Because he's going to depart in the service."

Evidently, the reason was peremptory.

"Well, listen, darling, you can't be the wife of a petty soldier under the flag. And then, one doesn't marry at that age and under those conditions. He must understand that."

He understands it perfectly...it's me who..."

A further lachrymal crisis, and Suzanne buried her pretty blonde head on her friend's shoulder.

What's wrong with her? What does she want? Perhaps she doesn't know very well herself. In very young and very ardent natures there are these desperate impatiences, these jibs, these revolts before a insurmountable obstacle, before the constant unrealisability of the slightest desire, the most innocent of dreams, whatever implications or social repercussions they might have, before the veto opposed to all our great passionate fevers, which invariably forbids us to do what we have a desperate desire to do, to attempt the only thing that we want to attempt.

"Think," she repeats, "that I'll be old in three years."

"Listen, then," says Gilberte, with a malicious smile, "it's certain that, in three years, we'll both be frightfully old—me especially, since I've already been waiting much longer than you, but look, I believe I have under my hand something that will ward off that nasty eventuality, and I want to enable you to profit from it."

"Oh! Speak, tell me, quickly."

"Monsieur d'Autremont, my brother and I are leaving tomorrow for an excursion in the desert and the mountains of Kaba, and we'll doubtless go as far as the Harward Institute."

Suzanne shivered, the pallor of an edelweiss stamped on her cheeks and temples, which she lifted up before Gilberte's eyes.

"I understand," she murmured. "You're going to ask him for his secret, his remedy against old age, but he won't give it to you...I know that, because I've begged him, I've dragged myself at his knees..."

"Ah! So you were the tearful young woman of the other evening...?"

"Shh! I don't know how you can have learned that, but it doesn't matter...listen, Gilberte, you're my friend, aren't you? Well, if you're really going out here, take me, I beg you. You'll see, the two of us will reckon with him, he'll deliver his secret to us; in your beautiful eyes of darkness and sunlight there's a fascination that he won't be able to resist."

Gilberte—who told me all about the scene afterwards—started laughing involuntarily. "If Monsieur d'Autremont could hear you!" But, having already become grave again, she added: "In any case, I'd better to tell you the truth right away...nothing in all this depends on me...the little voyage we're undertaking is, it seems, fatiguing; in addition, it involves certain risks. If the messieurs have decided to do it, it's evidently not for futile motives, but in view of a very serious, perhaps even secret, goal, and they wouldn't see a stranger getting involved without displeasure."

But nothing disconcerted the obstinate young woman.

"I'm not a stranger for Giuseppe, who has already paid court to me in his spare time in Nice."

"I don't know any moments that I wouldn't be disposed to spare for the same cause if I were a man. There remains Monsieur d'Autremont..."

"Oh, that one's so nice one can do anything one wants with him."

Further frank gaiety on the part of my Gilberte. "Thank you, that's reassuring; fortunately, I can count on the formal opposition of your parents to prevent you from suborning my excessively facile fiancé."

"That's exactly where you're deluded...and we'll have the proof of it right away."

The rest of the scene is played before Lucette and me.

"Maman! Maman! You felt sorry for me just now for being chagrined, so much chagrin, and you said to me in a fit of tender remorse...the tender remorse of intractable mothers who martyrize the hearts of their daughters in the name of some obsolete prejudice...you said that you didn't know what you could do to console me. Well, I know, and this is what you're going to do. Gilberte is departing with Monsieur Giuseppe and Monsieur d'Autremont for an excursion in the Kaba desert..."

"Truly!" cries Lucette. "You're going to savor life under the big tent!"

"Oh, only for one or two nights," said Gilberte, defensively.

"How I envy you! My husband claims that we're too old for those sorts of escapades, otherwise..."

Suzanne seized the ball in flight. "Oh, that's just like Papa! With him one is always too old or too young. That won't prevent you from obtaining from him this time that I can accompany Gilberte."

"You!"

"Yes, me! The contemplation of the great spaces is, it's said, an excellent remedy against cardiac crises…and then, my resignation is at that price."

Lucette reflects momentarily, and then "Perhaps you're right, great spoiled child; at your age it requires so little to forget…" She turns toward Gilberte. "All right; I'll take charge of extracting the master's consent…Suzanne is yours."

When we announce that news to Giuseppe—as has happened before—his face contracts and frowns as if under the effect of a violent chagrin. And I thought he was in love with little Saint-Marceau, at least within the limits that a businessman like him can be! Suddenly he has the heavy eyes, the half-squinting gaze that disfigures almost as much as it displaces the habitual lines of the face. In the moments, rare it is true, when Giuseppe's eyes undergo that torment, I have the impression of a different man than the one I know, that his family knows—but ordinarily, it passes so quickly that I forget to analyze it.

This time again it passes rapidly. Giuseppe contents himself with dating a glance at me that is simply reproving.

"How were you able to accept such a charge, to assume such a responsibility, at the risk of compromising the secret goal—which must remain secret—of our voyage? Suppose that Harward has emissaries here…"

I could tell him in good faith that his prejudice against Harward seems to me to be unjustified, that nothing authorizes us to suspect the scientist's actions and to treat him as an enemy, as long as he has not overtly taken a position against us, but that would take us too for and I prefer to get myself out of it with a quip.

"Insofar as it concerns me, I simply thought of giving you pleasure."

"You're joking. Suzanne is besotted with a young man who's leaving tomorrow to join the first chasseurs in the quality of a simple cavalier first class."

"All the more reason for making her forget him. For the rest...I have an idea that we'll reckon more easily with Harward, with whom I'll embark on negotiations alone, as a skilled diplomat..."

"We'll see...we'll see," says Giuseppe, brusquely. "Let's not make any premature decisions...one takes inspiration from circumstances...and advice from the leader of our escort."

This time, Gilberte and I start.

"An escort!" she says, nonplussed. "Do you really believe in the necessity of an escort?"

"It's *de rigueur* for crossing the desert. I've sought information in the consulates. It's customary to adjoin Sheikh Mohammed-ed-din, who resides in Kaba, and four indigenes from the tribe of the Allaouin, the most influential of the plain. They're reliable guides, whose flair of a hunting dog might be more useful to us than you think...in the mountains, at least.

I intervene, not without some scorn. "Bah! We'll have a companion who will surpass all of them in that regard...my dog Flax."

"Your dog!" Giuseppe almost bounds, while laughing to soften the effect of his ill humor. "How can you think of encumbering us with such impediments?"

But Gilberte takes up the cause of Flax, who has become her friend.

"Another dog might be an encumbrance, but not Flax...he's too sage, too intelligent. And then, I have an idea that his flair might tell us precisely what we're burning to know, furnishing us, even before we arrive at the Institute, with the material certainty of the presence or non-presence of Antonio in the establishment. This morning I made him sniff for a long time an object that belonged to the disappeared—a cravat—and already he appears to comprehend..."

"You've read that in the novels of Fenimore Cooper," sniggered Giuseppe. "In sum, all right for the pretty Suzanne and for Flax, but for the love of God don't produce any further complications for us between now and tomorrow, or I'll decline all responsibility. As for you, d'Autremont, if anything bad happens to your dog, you have only yourself to blame—taking a sheep-dog into the desert is pure folly...especially a briard...it's nervous, it can't stay still, it barks..."

"Never intemperately."

"It will attract wild beasts from a league around."

"Pooh! Jackals."

"Not to mention that it will pick quarrels with the douars' dogs."

"No, since I'll be there and he's habituated to listen-ing to his master's voice, which, I would say, he also puts a sort of humble joy into obeying, as if it were the best proof he can give me of his love and fidelity."

"All right, all right, I won't insist...I had to warn you about the risks you're running for your dog. Don't hold it against me; like you, I hope that everything goes well..."

When Giuseppe has gone Gilberte and I remain a little pensive. It is like a chagrined surprise that we dare not communicate to one another. We simply say that we had imagined Giuseppe to be more malleable, more in-clined to certain sensibilities—in sum, more inclined to certain sentiments that dominated both of us. But even so, we decide to take Flax.

XIII

We are at sea now aboard the little steam coaster *El Tih*, which is heading for Kaba, it's prow turned toward a barbaric sunset gilded in slices.

The Banchis have taken refuge in the lounge because of the swell. The worthy old couple insisted absolutely on accompanying Gilberte as far as the threshold of the desert, otherwise they would not have consented to confide her to us in such an impromptu fashion. Giuseppe, having become the most attentive and tender of nephews, is keeping them company, while Gilberte and I are attempting to catch a glimpse from the height of the poop of her balcony and my terrace: the balcony and the terrace where, scarcely a fortnight ago, we communicated for the first time at a distance. Suzanne is going from one group to the other, as happy as a schoolgirl in an escapade, but a trifle hermetic even so, like all young women of her age.

Already the details of the town are vanishing; Spalatrina is no longer anything but the tip of a wave darkening a pale décor of dream. Soon the entire cape seems to be fleeing under a storm-cloud, and in the livid dusk it suddenly takes on an aspect of an old undiscovered continent, over which the sadness of the first human ages is still floating.

Flax is sitting at my feet on his shiny black curly woolen backside. His superb ringed tail, slightly rough, also black and coiled around the hairy base, the inferior curve of which it espouses.

What is he thinking? The departure intrigued him, because it didn't resemble any other departure, and because I and Gilberte, his great friend, were surrounded by unfamiliar faces. A sensation of the provisional, the temporary, seems to be weighing upon him; doubtless he senses, by means of signs classified by his observant intelligence, everything ephemeral there is about the crossing. And perhaps he is anxious. Anxiety is in fact, the form in which the break in the continuity of his habits is translated in him, the interruption of the regular and consecrated phenomena that constitute the quotidian cycle of life.

Then too, he can discern perfectly the coast following us to our left: its flat yellow line, the little tongues of sand fringed with foam, the sudden projection of a promontory, a reef or a clump of palm trees. All that unknown solicits him and worries him, even at a distance, and he would prefer to see us set a course for the open sea, which would signify a return to the land from which he comes, the imminent end of unfamiliar horizons, uncertain boards and all the alerts the disturb his nervous centers.

But here comes the night—an appeasement for him as for us—and, confident in the petty providence that I incarnate in his eyes, he will go to sleep, since I am going to sleep and not afraid of anything.

That night only lasts a few hours, for we have gone to bed as late as possible because of the "discomfort," as Giuseppe puts it, of the cabins.

In truth, I have hardly slept. Since yesterday, perhaps for several days, a strange suspicion has awakened deep within me, stimulated by the increasingly inexplicable attitude of Giuseppe. I have tried hard, I have submitted to severe scrutiny the doubts that obsess me, but nothing appears to me to be natural, not to say coherent, in his personality. I cannot say that I suspect his good faith, the sincerity of the evidence of affection that he lavishes on Gilberte and the camaraderie with which he honors me; I dare not put in doubt either his loyalty nor his evident desire to help us to put an end the mystery of Antonio's disappearance, and yet...

And yet, for several days I've been experiencing a kind of malaise in his presence, a malaise that must have existed in a latest state for a long time, to the impact of which I might perhaps have submitted as soon as our first encounter. Yes, certainly, if I integrate memories still recent, I can't forbid myself the certainty that I had, since the beginning, a sort of suspicion in his regard, an unreasoning, inconsistent suspicion, only perceived in the skin.

Perhaps his slightly closed face made a bad impression on the psychologist slumbering within me?

Today, as I analyze that face feature by feature, I can only incriminate the eyes, those heavy eyes whose eyelids sometimes seem incapable of lifting If they are lifted by surprise, they reveal a gaze completely different from the one expected, given the cordiality of the words pronounced by the mouth, the bonhomie or affability of the intonations: a gaze that jars with that mouth and its wheedling inflections; a gaze that would be that of the great raptors if it were not filtered in spite of everything by a human eye.

Perhaps I'm going too far; that's the danger of imprecise suspicions; one doesn't know where they stop. The only thing of which I'm very certain today is that I'm experiencing increasing difficulty in continuing my sympathy for Giuseppe. Perhaps I've never veritably accorded it to him, at any moment.

XIV

The imposing aspect of Kaba, or Beït-Kaba, the ancient Turkish fortress straddling the frontier of Syria and Egypt, at the foot of which the south-western tip of the desert of Petra ends, has been greatly praised to us. At the moment when our steamboat drops anchor in the bay, the sun roses over a décor that suggests to my Gilberte a citation from Lamartine, the great pilgrim of Syria; but I am too preoccupied to savor its charm.

A blast of the khamsin, the desert wind, has been predicted, and I wish that we were on land, for the bay is dangerous even in ordinary weather. However, the steam-launch that is coming to collect us reassures me immediately regarding a disembarkation that was once made on a man's back. Now I am tranquil enough to welcome the rather violent solicitations—everything is raw white for the moment—of the landscape. There I, in fact, before us a kind of landslide of low cupolas and terraces emerging from a confusion of white walls whose reverberation is blinding.

That first aspect of Kaba is very engaging thanks to the exposure of the terraces and the fine aerial reliefs that all Oriental landscapes borrow from the perfect purity of the atmosphere and the admirable melting of horizons. Unfortunately, the calcined land all around immediately comes to spoil that welcoming impression, and the desolate character of the surroundings—the gardens of Kaba are not perceptible from the sea—reveal for the first time to us, as Spalatrians, the accursed land of Palestine.

That, in any case, as you will see, is one of the least disappointments that await the voyager.

To the north and south of Kaba the eye embraces nothing but sand dunes. Red toward the strand, white everywhere else, especially toward the south, where the desert of Petra opens, which separates Palestine from Egypt. At intervals, there is an Arab hamlet, a dozen miserable huts made from dry mud with straw roofs. That is the plain of Sharon, which extends all along the coast from Petra to Carmel. It is the same country that scripture represents as an extraordinarily rich and fertile land covered with preciously perfumed plants.

In spring, in fact, the valley fills up spontaneously with flowers. One encounters tulips, roses, cloves, anemones, yellow lilies and white lilies, the famous lily of Sharon whose splendor Jesus praised by comparing it to Solomon in all his glory. At the beginning of the bad season, that beautiful vegetation disappears to give way to thistles; the plain of Sharon is then no more than one more desert in a land that has so many.

While I glorify myself before Gilberte and Suzanne in that facile erudition collected from a guide, we each land, and it is the abomination of desolation. Kaba resembles every other décor of the Levant; as soon as one approaches it one distinguishes the muddy coating of the colors, the cracks, the bumps and the infamous soiling of the frame. The port is nothing more than a dirty street strewn with filth and detritus of every sort, bordered on the sea by ruined wall facing a serpentine line of sordid and wretched houses. Inside, there is a confusion of mariners, camels, Arabs wearing all kinds of costumes, and English tourists with green veils, which constitutes all the animation of Kaba. That host of men and animals emerges from a mountainous street that divides into several conduits passing under vaults and arcades; that is Kaba's bazaar. That bazaar itself ends in the great market square, where camels pullulate.

Saddled and bridled donkeys, long-tailed sheep and superb Bedouins on horseback armed to the teeth cut through the hedges of merchants displaying in the open air bread, fruits, vegetables and brightly colored fabrics, all with a great reinforcement of guttural exclamations.

Single story shacks resembling our drying-sheds, a bizarre tangle of blackened beams, which one might think saved from a conflagration, loom up at the back; they are cafés. The terraces are garnished by muslims squatting on the ground or sitting on stools, who drink their coffee while smoking narghiles or chibouks.

Muslim and Armenian women clad in ample white batiste, their faces veiled in black or fragments of floral-patterned calico like the kerchiefs of our peasants, traverse the scene slowly and silently, with the embarrassed gait lent to them by the trouser-skirts with large pleats worn by all Arab women. The white cloth that envelops them entirely falls all the way to the ankles, in such a way as only to allow the feet to be seen. The consequence of that is that all the exterior coquetry of those women is concentrated in their footwear. Their shoes generally have high heels, of fine leather with arabesques, elegantly arched...the heels of the mysterious malefactress who assassinated Lord Cattledown!

We traverse the heart of the town to reach the Consuls Hotel, where our rooms are booked. The narrow and smoky streets, with overhanging stories, are linked by stairways of black stone, sticky and half-collapsed. Rotten rags are drying on arched balconies.

Such streets are simple vaulted passages, cluttered with filth, which resemble sewers deflected from their original usage. Everywhere, life seems immobilized and stagnant, struck in the same sources. The pretty Moorish houses that one sees in the distance are shaky edifices open to all the winds, sketches of houses, destined to remain eternally unfinished, and which do, in fact, offer indentations of shadow and emptiness, the dilapidated nudities characteristic of buildings under construction.

On the eastern side, above all, the town takes on the appearance of a sacked fortress. Crumbling ramparts protrude, set against a huge mound of mud, which covers the place where the old public ditches have been recently filled in, and which resembles a collapsed bastion itself. Naked children play from morning until evening in all that ordure and dust, pell-mell with stray dogs with yellow fur and the faces of hyenas, bastardized descendants of the famous jackals that Solomon employed to carry fie into the Philistine camp.

I impart that Biblical reminiscence to Gilberte and Suzanne, who appreciate it at its true value. It remains a dead letter for Flax, for we see him salute those degenerates in passing, very affably, as he salutes all the ordinary members of his species, his vulpine head apparently scaring the too much for them to return his politeness.

At the hotel we disband. The Banchi couple need a few hours rest; the demoiselles request permission to change their clothes. Giuseppe departs in search of his escort on the heels of a big fellow, who truly has a grandiose air in his burnoose, with his tanned face, his tiger's eyes, his spurred boots and the weapons that hang all over him.

"He's Mohammed-ed-din, the most powerful sheikh in the desert," Giuseppe whispered to me as he left. "He understands a few words of English, and as he has a *pied-à-terre* here, I'm going home with him to discuss our escort with him; if he agrees to serve as our guide, we can be tranquil."

I'm obliged to recognize that Giuseppe's prudence is neither as outré nor as inopportune as I thought. On seeing all the desert Arabs circulating here, armed to the teeth, one is immediately edified regarding the mores in honor among the Bedouins of the plain, and Giuseppe has acted with the sage prudence of a man who has been in the country before.

I watch him go away and I admire once again his prodigious gifts of assimilation, for it is quite familiarly that he is already circulating in these back-streets that he did not know two hours ago. And yet, that ends up leaving me, perhaps unreasonably, with a malaise that does not increase my confidence in him.

We have spent the afternoon visiting the famous gardens that extend along the road to Egypt, a veritable forest of orange trees, which strew the ground with an odorous snow, the perfume of which, this morning, welcomes us in a full tide. Figs, lemons and pomegranates also grow; their foliage forms low vaults, into which aloes and giant cacti insert their maleficent spines, and which are framed by hedges of myrtle or jasmine.

In Indian file, with the dog bringing up the rear, we are gliding through an atmosphere heavy with unusual aromas, a silent phantasmagorical penumbra. The hour is exquisite, and Suzanne makes us appreciate the charm with droll remarks, sometimes a trifle risqué but perfectly adequate to her sprightly allure, ignorant of all constraint and any timidity. I suspect her to have a curious and ardent young soul. similar to her face, already burnished, exoticized by the force of ambiences, a soul steeped in the fiery sunlight of a dream, a dream, as ardent and imperious as all of her young person, unable either to resign herself or to wait.

When we return to the hotel Giuseppe announces to us that we will depart tomorrow morning at dawn, if we are firmly determined to execute the raid of which he is not a partisan, to which he will only attach himself reluctantly. Our silence is a tacit confirmation of our unshakable determination, and he then praises the proud allure of the four Bedouin horsemen who will serve as our escort under the command of Mohammed-ed-din, who has agreed to do us the honor of accompanying us in person.

Thus, the die is cast. We dine comfortably, and at seven o'clock, after a scene of farewell slightly saddened by the tears shed on either side—even Giuseppe has red eyes—we embark the old Banchis, who are taking the mail-boat to Jaffa in order to get home more rapidly. Then we separate, with the firm intention of sleeping as much as possible; at least, I have obtained from Gilberte and Suzanne that they will go to bed, in anticipation of tomorrow's fatigues, and the sleepless nights that might await us.

Personally, I sense that I won't sleep tonight; all those Bedouin faces obsess my imagination, and I ask myself once again whether it might not be better to have ourselves conveyed by the cares of the Cook agency.

However, Giuseppe must have acted for the best, and in that respect, at least, his shrewd zeal, and all the trouble he has taken on our behalf, cannot be criticized. In any case, our ships are burned, there is nowhere to go but forwards.

From the height of the hotel terrace, I witness a dazzling dusk that, at least for a few minutes, almost makes me forget where I am. The rare palm trees of the coast suddenly stand out in the magical solitude of the sky, designing their fine black lace against a background of crimson and gold. Under a rain of golden darts, the sea, like changing silk, is tinted with mysterious green clarities, an electric green like that of fireworks; the breeze runs gently over the waves and goes all the way to the horizon, creasing and unfurling impalpable luminous gauzes. The city falls asleep, as if drowned in a heavy atmosphere of perfumes, the ardor of its white walls extinguished.

Now, the terraces facing me, all the white crenellations, stacked and pressed against the sky, become animated. Silhouettes of women appear, isolated in the immense aerial décor, populating alone all the immensity of the tableau. An Arab woman appears, without veils, in a pretty pink costume, an ashen light blurring her delicate profile, neatly cutting out her svelte figure in a light devoid of horizons. She makes a gesture, and that gesture usurps all the interest of the spectacle, and the sky appears less desert and the sea less vast; other apparitions surge forth between the rounded domes of the nearby cupolas...

But now, close by, barely fifteen meters as the crow flies, on a terrace that two or three streets must nevertheless separate from the hotel, one of those gracious phantoms appears to have taken me for a focal point of attention, for at the same time as her gestures adjure me, the two eyes that surmount the horizontal stripe of the veil, alone alive in all that white linen, remained fixed on me with a grim tenacity that troubles me.

Her most frequent gesture raises a horrified palm toward the desert, a palm that curses and repels, and then, with the same hand, she indicates the sky, and then the desert again; then the two hands come together in order to come apart almost immediately in a violent detachment.

And she recommences, untiringly, while the shadows thicken between her and me, only to cease, finally, when the dense night has almost dissolved and abolished her silhouette.

With the night, the predicted khamsin has fallen upon the city, and is literally suffocating. I lie down on a mat in order to dream. What did that unknown woman want of me, with her troubling mime? And those eyes, which still pursue me, and which are not entirely unknown to me! For truly, eyes have a unique expression for every being. Isolated from the individual to whom they belong, they remain recognizable, because they have a personality, a physiognomy of their own, independent of the features of the face.

But it does not matter, for although I am sure that I know those phantom eyes, I cannot tell where I have seen them before.

And I end up going to sleep, until the moment when I feel my shoulder touched.

A cold violent dawn has replaced the night, and I must still be under the influence of yesterdays evening's vision, for scarcely have I opened my eyes than I perceive the Moorish eyes fixed upon me, grim and prophetic.

Bah! They are Giuseppe's eyes. Astonished to find me sleeping in the open, while congratulating himself for not having to hasten my toilette, he says: "The camels and mules are ready, the guides too, and we're only waiting for the demoiselles."

I hasten to tell him about my aerial adventure of the previous evening. He bursts out laughing.

"Either you've had a nightmare or you've made—quite involuntarily, I'm sure—the conquest of some neighborhood houri whose telegraphic signals you've misinterpreted."

"I assure you…"

But he does not even give me time to explain. "Listen…where is this terrace?"

I indicate it to him without the lightest hesitation, having take sufficient reference-points the previous evening.

"Good, it's only a few paces away. We have no time to waste, but I want to have a clear heart. Give me two minutes."

And he's gone. His absence is brief, in fact. He comes back accompanied by Sheikh Mohammed, who is speaking to him volubly in a low voice, which only obtains from him, by way of reply, discouraged shrugs of the shoulders.

"Well," says Giuseppe, breaking that bizarre conversation, the house crowned by the terrace in question is entirely uninhabited, abandoned several months ago, hence the impossibility of resolving the enigma in the sense of a gallant apparition, not to say any apparition of flesh and bone. Thus, you remain afflicted and convinced of having had a nightmare, unless we admit the hypothesis of our sheikh."

"What hypothesis?"

"That of a kind of incarnate spirit. You know that there is a strong analogy between some of our spirit phenomena and those of Arab occultism. The sheik has told me that a young Syrian woman from Beirut tried to cross the desert of Petra alone a few months ago. She fell afoul of bandits, and since then has sometimes appeared to voyagers ready to follow the same route, in order to try to dissuade them from departing. What do you think of that?"

It's so absurd that I'm not even tempted to laugh. I turn the question on Giuseppe. "What do you think of it?"

"In placing myself on superstitious terrain, of course, I can only remind you of my personal apprehensions, the efforts I made to turn you away from this journey, from which I expect nothing good in any manner, and repeat to you that there is still time to renounce it, if your confidence in the final outcome is as fragile as mine."

The dark Moorish gaze—for Giuseppe definitely has Moorish eyes—plunge into my gaze with a kind of searching emotion, but I hold firm, not understanding this stubborn pessimism, bordering on cowardice. I ask one last question.

"Have you any doubt regarding the quality of our escort?"

"None."

"Then let's go. Anyway, here are the demoiselles, helmeted and booted, and I'll wager that they wouldn't renounce utilizing their prestigious amazon outfits in tussore silk for anything in the world."

"You've said it," ratifies Suzanne promptly, who has only heard the last words, "and it's necessary not to try to make us wear our vile homespun garments again. Look what a fine appearance Gilberte has on her black mule."

In fact, Gilberte is already in the saddle, and while watching my own movements tenderly, she continues a very animated conversation with Flax, who jumps up at her legs.

115

In the meantime, our escort has mounted the camels; only the sheikh is on horseback, for the sake of decorum. The desert runners are five in number, four for the guides and one for the baggage. The last is enormous, and never ceases whining, as if everything inconveniences it, including its hump. While it collapses, bending its knees, in order to receive its burden, its Asiatic eye has that fixed laughter, by means of which one does not know whether it is sad or cheerful, and it is with an impassive disdain that it sniffs in passing the two mares that are brought for Giuseppe and me.

The little caravan sets forth at a jolly trot, under a rain of guttural vociferations that ricochet singularly in the silence of the city, still asleep.

XV

The road that we take as soon as we emerge from the ruined ramparts is a broad swath of sand incessantly traversed by large lizards whose furtive movements are the only alerts in the landscape—a melancholy landscape, the horizons of which are nevertheless luminous, closed in the distance, toward the north-east, by the blue screens of the Djebel-el-Tih.

From time to time we cross the path of some Arab vagabond draped in a wretched brown-striped plaid, coiffed by a twisted kerchief and shod in rotten sandals, sometime simple palm-bark soles crudely attached to the foot with string.

The sun is not yet visible, but one senses that out there, behind the mountains of the Levant, a diabolical frying is in preparation, and we hold our breath in order not to inhale excessively the furnace blasts that the wings of the khamsin are already delegating to us.

Giuseppe has taken the lead with the sheikh; I am riding between Gilberte to my right and Suzanne to my left; the mounted camels are bringing up the rear.

It is not the desert, properly speaking, the sand sea of the Africa Sahara, but it is at least a land of sinister solitude, where geographical surprises, which would be pleasant anywhere else, invariably take on an aspect of bleak desolation.

All the accidents of the terrain, as far as the eye can see, have the dismal fixity of the stone in which they are carved; the wild places and the tormented horizons follow one another and resemble one another. Some gorge or sinister valley, an end of which is glimpsed in the gap of the preceding gorge, seems to promise marvels, but only continue to repeat the landscape one has just quit— and it is so lacking in verdure. We follow little thalwegs that are only the dry beds of as many streams, little laby- rinthine gorges devoid of shadow or mystery, all marl or hard clay, rock or gypsum, with gray salt or calcined plaster.

Suzanne is amused by everything, by the hostile and forbidding air of the smallest valley, by the Bedou- ins we encounter, who dart inexpressible glances at us, by a jackal that runs away like a hare, by the grimace of a camel, by the fleeting silhouette of some wild pig.

Gilberte is graver. At certain times she even seems to be oppressed by something other than the implacable sun and the overwhelming sky, the curve of which launches so high and so profound from the edge of the devastated horizon. Perhaps she is trying to imagine An- tonio's impressions when he rids her of all the burden of her sinister promise, with the bitter desire to make that route the final stage of normal life.

We are almost sure now that he has passed this way. Flax, who sometimes sniffs the cravat again at length, is as grave and meditative as Gilberte herself, and his nose, at times, almost trails on the ground, as he trots obliquely, with abrupt pauses and resumptions of frenet- ic impetus of a dog following an arduous and difficult trail.

After so many years! you one might think; but it is necessary to remember that we are on the threshold of Arabia Petraea, the only point on the globe where every- thing is immutable, because everything there participates in the rigidity of death, the millennial abandonment of the soil. If a stone falls there, among the thistles, it has every chance of remaining there until the end of the world. Thus, the traces of a caravan, especially the odorous atoms of a trail, endure, for certain senses of smell, for as long as the properties of a magnet or the inexhaustible emanations of radium.

Of course, I have not spoken to Gilberte about the incident of the terrace; on the contrary, I shall avoid carefully any depressing impression during this journey, which might put our energy to a rude proof. In any case, our progress at the moment is fast enough to prevent any coherent conversation; it is a matter of attaining the little oasis of Aïn-Namur before the torrid midday. The heat is already such that we all have brick-red tints beneath our white headgear.

To the north-east, in the direction of Gaza, a group of tents puts a leprous brown patch on the ground. There is not another soul between there and the place where the breast of the prophet erects its white nipple, isolated in the sky.

To the north, toward Petra, there is the Djebel-el-Tih dominating a whole group of spectral summits; closer, rocks are accumulated, immobile, mute and sun-baked, raising narrow avenues of refracted fire, amphitheaters of low, naked hills with cheese-like cliffs—the bulbous dome of a koubba glittering in the verdure—and, floating above all those things, the slow, heavy, magnetic fight of a eagle, an old local marabout, for whom the caravans that pass by are sometimes more of a windfall than an alarming inconvenience.

As we advance further toward the north-east, the peak of the Djebel-el-Tih reappears more frequently above the ridges that hide it from us. It is obsessive, that peak, lavish and multiple, invading the background of all the tableaux, like a miniature Fujiyama. It shows itself to the right, then to the left, then ahead, then behind, under all the aspects that a peak of that nature can take, looming up in the full sun of Asia, in the deep azure of a fiery sky. For it is more triumphant than ever, that incandescent Baal. It expands in all its splendor of a despotic idol, and the poor earth, into the entrails of which it delves, lies at its feet, dazzled, breathless and suffocated. Everything that moves on its surface experiences the same vertigo, the same crushing, and the same self-abandonment.

Our speed has accelerated; we are galloping in a furnace through the general blaze of things toward a region that we divine to be even more fiery, even more burning. And now there is a swarming in the distance, directly ahead of us.

Animals! As long as they aren't buffaloes…no…they're sheep changing oases.

A few minutes later we plunge into the fleecy waves, which close round us, a tangle of frightened, bewildered heads and trampling feet, while pile up and draw apart, just enough to avoid the hooves of our mounts. The thick warmth that rises from that population of animals completes the furnace of the air, the temperature suddenly becoming intolerable, and lost in the bosom of those pullulating fleeces, we have the sensation of some infernal kitchen in which living sheep pass directly from their natural form to the state of roasted cutlets.

"Oof!" says Suzanne, when we emerge intact from the last waves of the flock. "They only lack a little garlic!"

And they draw way, the poor victims of Baal, swarming and simmering, on the road, carrying with them the atmosphere of their own coking, perhaps consoling themselves with the idea that the big half-naked fellow leading them will be grilled before they will.

Here is the oasis, the refuge of this stage of the journey. It is behind a curtain of long plumed reeds, a vast triangular marsh in which herons, teal, pelicans, ducks, etc., are frolicking freely, as well as a dozen buffaloes watched by a young pastor, whose dirty half-burnoose allows the sight of two gingerbread legs.

At the extreme tip of the triangle, a delightful surprise, near an old ruined caravanserai guarded by a bashi-bazouk occupied in knitting a sock, a grove of olive-trees, cork-oaks, oleanders and banana-trees opens, here we can pitch our tents while our animals slake their thirst at the springs that can be heard rippling everywhere. The camping equipment is unpacked, the folding beds and the thick woolen blankets.

"Agree," I say to Giuseppe, who had come back to us, "that we would have been wrong to allow ourselves to be discouraged. "One can find everything in this amusing desert, this fake Sahara guarded by gendarmes. One can even find champagne!" And, triumphantly, I show him the little case that I had slipped surreptitiously into the provisions.

He smiles in a somewhat constrained manner, only finding vague and reticent circumlocutions to oppose me. One might think that his skepticism is increasing in proportion to our enthusiasm.

I also observe that, since this morning, he has not looked me in the face once. There is definitely something amiss...and what troubles me most of all is that I am the only one to have divined it, and cannot confide my intuitions to anyone.

A solid meal and a long siesta take us as far as five o'clock. We resume our route then, only stopping at nightfall, at El-Djera, a wretched little Turkish fort, which one might think besieged by the surrounding Bedouin encampments.

A short night, and not very enchanting, at El-Djera.

On awakening, at four o'clock, a big surprise—worse than a surprise, a disagreeable alarm. The four cameleers of our escort have disappeared, along with their mounts, only leaving us the baggage camel. I seek advice from Sheikh Mohammed, who is lamenting verbosely in an almost infantile pidgin.

He does not understand anything. Nothing similar has ever happened in the twenty years that he has been guiding tourists in the desert—he is forty years old. He is dishonored, and he offers immediately to return the payments we have made him. His despair seems sincere, and what is strange about the affair is that he swears by Allah that the cameleers were not hired by him personally. By whom then?

I observe Giuseppe; he simply seems consternated, and when he finally raises his eyes to me, his gaze simply expresses the unique thought: What do we do now?

I interrogate Mohammed.

"Do you think it necessary to recruit a new escort from among the Bedouins of the nearby encampment?"

"They'll skin you, and besides which, they aren't Allaouin, and in consequence, I can't answer for them."

"Are you strong enough to conduct us safe and sound to the foot of the mountain?"

"On my head."

"The let's continue our route."

Giuseppe looks suffocated; he was counting firmly on our retracing our steps.

"You know," he said, "I wash my hands of it. However, and with the sole aim of covering your responsibility, which from now on is solely in play"—he emphasizes those words—"you ought perhaps to consult the opinion of the demoiselles."

"It's done! They've given me carte blanche."

And I turn my back on him, his cowardice finally inspiring in me a sentiment close to scorn.

I help the sheikh to load our tents and baggage on the only camel that remains to us, and we set forth again

This time the landscape changes. We're approaching the north-eastern limit of the part of the desert that separates us from Djebel-el-Tih. In the depths of the sky a sequence of gigantic tents is outlined: the blue mountains of Palestine. Hillocks surge forth everywhere, which all bear traces of human activity and genius, but of a humanity so remote that scarcely any record of it other than the Old Testament.

The majority of the vestiges of art in the midst of which we are moving belong to the funerary genre. I try to palliate the lugubrious character of Gilberte's and Suzanne's eyes by feeding them a few historic memories.

"To think that this isolated country was once inhabited by a flourishing nation, the Nabaateans, I believe."

"Doubtless a nation of marble-workers," Suzanne jokes.

In fact, one might think it the ruins of a city of tombs and mausolea, in the process of the excavation of delicately-chiseled orifices, monumental friezes and haut- and bas-reliefs sculpted in the rock.

Soon we traverse a meandering gorge emerging in giant rocks with walls riddled with sculpted holes, which are nothing but ancient niches for coffins. They make one dream of a race of Titans who, arrested by death in their supreme ascension, hollowed out their tombs in the same sheer slopes by means of which they had counted on scaling the clouds, in order to die as close as possible to the gods they had hoped to dethrone.

"Well," says Giuseppe, "It's not cheerful here. Fortunately, we're nearly at the end of our journey, for these are the first foothills of the Djebel-el-Tih, and this evening, after the siesta, we'll be able to attempt the ascent. It only remains for me to congratulate you, for your fine audacity has reckoned with my prudence."

As he finishes speaking, rifle shots ring out to our right, two hundred meters ahead of the small group that we form at the foot of the sandstone mound that marks the exit from the funereal defile

The idea of an ambush chills my marrows, while I throw myself uselessly in front of Gilberte and Suzanne. But this time I have to praise Giuseppe's admirable sang-froid, and also his courage. He takes their two mules behind a rocky spur and races forward himself at a gallop. Mohammed follows him, pale, his eyes glittering, his finger on the trigger of his carbine. I rejoin them, after making sure that our companions are in a safe place.

In the distance, in the fleecy smoke, three or four cavaliers are leading a diabolical fantasia, burnooses and manes flying, and every time their gallop brings them almost in front of us, a shot is fired.

"Don't fire!" Giuseppe cries to Mohammed, whose horse is rearing up. "It's a simple demonstration; they're firing in the air to intimidate us, but we'll know why."

And he spurs his horse so furiously that it bounds forward frenetically, with Flax at his heels. I launch forward in my turn, followed by Mohammed, but the fantasia ceases, as if by enchantment, our aggressors veering away abruptly and disappearing behind an elbow of the mountain.

XVI

Gilberte and Suzanne have been very bold. We find them on foot, sheltered behind their mules, revolvers in hand.

Now we pepper the sheikh with rapid and precise questions. What does he think about that? He doesn't think anything at all, poor fellow, he's stupefied, bewildered, and once again, his confusion seems to me to be sincere.

"In any case," he explains, "They're not Allaouin, although my douar is less than a league from here. I would have recognized them. I think they're more likely to be the Arabs of our escort, in which case they'll pay dearly."

"But they didn't have horses," objected Gilberte, swiftly.

"They might have procured some since their flight. Deep down, there's a mystery in all this that it's necessary to clarify."

A strange gleam lights up in the frank eyes of the sheikh, obstinately fixed on Giuseppe—who finally shrugs his shoulders and declares the incident closed. Mohammed then offers us hospitality in his douar, situated at the foot of the mountain—where, he adds, the demoiselles can rest for as long as they please.

I hasten to accept, in order to draw the assent of the versatile Giuseppe, whose hesitant, irresolute air appears to offend our sheikh.

The arrival of a group of Allaouin Bedouins who come to meet us, attracted by the rifle fire, cuts the matter short definitively and we depart again, this time under a good escort.

"Something bad is good," Giuseppe says. "The simulacrum of aggression of which we've been the victims will serve our plan of campaign. My opinion is that you should present yourself at the Institute with the two young women and request that Harward grants them hospitality by reason of the peril that they've run, and which they still appear to be running. Gilberte, of course, will keep her incognito temporarily. As for you, their chaperon, with whom Harward has already consented to an interview, you'll evidently benefit from the same favors as them. Harward can't avoid that without lacking the strictest humanitarian duties. Once inside, it's up to you to devote yourself to adroit and patient investigations, the success of which doesn't seem to me to be in doubt. You'll take your time, of course, without any abruptness."

"All right, but what about you?"

"I'll stay under cover to begin with, for we've forgotten one thing: my resemblance to Antonio, which will render any subterfuge vain and consequently determine Harward to get rid of us, one way or another."

"That's reasonable. What will you do, then?"

"Don't worry about me. Arab hospitality isn't a vain word, and I'm convinced that Mohammed will be happy and proud to have me as a guest for as long as you judge it necessary to remain at the Institute. And as you won't be a prisoner there nothing will prevent you from keeping me up to date with the progress of your delicate enquiry."

Giuseppe's plan is perfect this time, foreseeing everything, providing for everything, based on the most logical probabilities. I approve of it all the more because it will doubtless rid us of him for some time, delivering me at the same stroke from the muted suspicion in his regard for which I reproach myself.

"Let's go; first thing tomorrow we'll give Gilberte and Suzanne their lesson…but Harward knows Suzanne, since he refused her his assistance the other evening. Let her persevere in her insanity; she'll play her role more naturally, and Gilberte, under an assumed name, will simply pass for having been towed along by that childish caprice by virtue of amity."

I have just finished regulating the details of that impromptu with Gilberte when we reach the oasis, our final stop.

It's pretty, the oasis of Mezraa, with its murmurous springs, the dense black freshness of its natural orchards, all the more cheerful because the fold in the mountain in which it is nestled inclines the contrast of its sepulchral niches above us. The inferior buttresses of that polymorphic mass of sandstone still remain green, wild pears, almonds and olives, and then oaks, growing there in profusion, while the higher slopes, completely bare but sculpted, for the most part, some into porticos and columns, suspend above the soft green cloak the friezes and severe frontons of a vast aerial necropolis.

It is a sort of memento mori situated at an altitude that only advertisements for Swiss chocolate surpass today. And it's behind that funereal geography that Harward has retrenched his Institute.

There are many more tents than fixed huts in Mohammed's douar, for three-quarters of the Allaouin are nomadic pastors; only the agricultural minority is sedentary. That sector furnishes the Harward Institute with vegetables and cereals, and renews the establishment's food supplies at determined intervals.

Brave men all, since guarded, or nearly so; there are still one or two forts on the edge of the desert, not to mention the citadel of Kerak, three days march from there. Superfluous precautions, in any case, for the cultivation of onions and shallots—which grow wild in that corner of the world, which is, I believe their cradle—softens mores at least as much as music, of which those desert people are fond, even though their ears cannot appreciate semitones.

My knowledge of an ex-globetrotter permits me to explain all that to Suzanne while we plunge alone into a little nearby wood in quest of a place to chat at our ease. Gilberte, fatigued, is asleep in her tent, Giuseppe has departed hunting, and Suzanne seems to have some confidence to impart to me.

At first we paddle in the intersecting beds of weak streams; she tucks up her skirts as if to pass over a ford, showing the lace of her underskirt, with hues of rare plumage, her legs ill-assured among the pebbles, going around pools with the precaution of a wading bird. Seen from the side she seems to have a child-like grace that jars with the already-full curves of her young body with her thin forehead of a woman hemmed with a prodigious blonde shell. And a womanly sadness also shines in her child-like gaze, where two periwinkles languish that ought to be blossoming in the sun.

A false step has just thrown her against my shoulder. She smiles and apologizes, and as our amused eyes met, the concern that is tormenting her finally pours out; doubtless her sagacity has detected in me am indulgent and discreet gentleman.

She says: "For several days I've been burning to know your sincere opinion on the step that I attempted with regard to Professor Harward, and which I count on renewing tomorrow."

I am forced to admit that I do not have one, and for good reason; I only know about that step the little that Gilberte has told me. I arm myself with ironic banter.

"I confess, dear little friend, that I don't understand very well the kind of hope that you're putting in Harward, with regard to a matter that escapes his habitual speculations: Amour."

"But since you know my…case, and you've been told that he possesses a sovereign remedy against old age, or rather against aging…"

"Three years don't count at your age."

"You think that…add three years to the age of Cleopatra and you'd change the face of the world more surely than modifying the tip of her nose."

"All right, I plead incompetence. A graver question poses itself: do you really know of what Professor Harward's remedy consists?"

"Yes, and I'll tell you…in fact, no, I can't…it's a secret…I've sworn…"

"Feminine oaths are made to be broken…"

"It's you who says that…finally, so be it. It's thanks to my young friend, little Doppendale, whose father is presently under treatment at the Institute, that I know all that."

"All what."

"The remedy simply consists of suspending life temporarily in the patient."

"By what means?"

"Oh, that's what I don't know…that's what no one can tell me…but Miss Doppendale affirms that, according to her father, the means is radical."

"Good. Your secret doesn't weigh much, and you'll easily brave the remorse of having betrayed it. Believe me, there's only one sure means of arresting life and, subsequently, the effects of its usury, and that's death."

"You're lugubrious…! How good it smells, the smoke escaping from those primitive chimneys!"

"Yes, the mere fact of being alive, at your age, is a multiple joy at every moment. You'd do well to remember that, for you don't know whether Harward's remedy is dangerous, a redoubtable chimera, and whether the subjects whose life he suspends thus don't lose, permanently, the faculty of living."

Pensive, or simply sullen, Suzanne inclines her face toward the ground and—as often before—I am confused by the morbid mystery that weighs upon the critical age of young women. How can it be explained that this one wants to risk death for a petty young man whose intimate depths she surely does not know? I try to console her.

"It's necessary, before all, to live, my dear Suzanne. Loving only comes afterwards, long afterwards, for loving is a fashion of dying. There's no need, therefore, for a Harward in this affair; in order not to grow old you merely have to cease loving without rhyme or reason, above all without security, at a junction in life when all is only illusion."

"Oh! What about you?"

"Gilberte and I have aged," I say, swelling with pride.

"What should I do, then?" she murmurs, her hands dangling, with no concern for her skirts, which have fallen back and are dipping into the water of the wadi.

I hesitate momentarily—for fear of cauterizing the wound in that childish heart too brutally, and then:

"Simply wait, and have faith in your mother, who will be the best and most reliable of guides for you."

"Why wait, why put aside happiness, ordinarily so ungraspable, when it is offered by chance?"

"Happiness is everywhere; it's happy people that are rare. In order to be happy, it's necessary to be able to wait."

Suzanne has stopped walking. A pink cloud invades the delicate paste of her face, reaches the little bulging forehead, and evaporates.

The pink cloud is the smoke of the battle that is being delivered inside her. Now that I've informed her, without knowing very much, about the etiology of her case and the true remedy it requires, she knows what it remains for her to do, and how hard it is. She knows what determination to make, that it is necessary first to put a lock on her inconsistent dream of amour, a dream condemned, in order to set a course for a definitive elsewhere, but she hesitates...dolorously.

Then, suddenly, she takes my arm, and, with a laugh that sounds clearly under the bushy church of orchards: "Let's go and wake Gilberte; I need her to encourage my...conversion."

This time, I'm tranquil. Suzanne will make honorable amends to Harward, who will no longer have any reason to suspect the poor stranded tourists that we are. And once inside the place..."

XVII

At dawn, which is very cool here, we are up and about, in conference with Mohammed, who explains our itinerary on the mountain.

There are two paths, one impracticable for us, which leads straight to the Institute in an hour and a half via steep short cuts, veritable chimneys, climbs for ibex or young Arabs, where mules cannot pass. That is the road followed by the Allaouin porters on the days when they renew the supplies of the great scientific establishment. The other route, a real muleteers' road, is much easier, but it represents five long hours of ascents and descents.

In fact, three or for medium-sized peaks circle and dominate the aerial terrace where the Institute is situated, which forms a kind of gigantic balcony on the flank of the superior massif of Djebel-el-Tih. Instead of slipping between those peaks, as the short cuts does, the road follows the lesser profiles on a ledge that scales them in zigzags ad then descends again every time into the hollows of the intermediate valleys before climbing again.

"But you'll have the advantage," observes Mohammed, still in his pidgin English, "of not having to dismount and not going astray. Furthermore, I'll give you a reliable guide, my young son..."

He makes sure that Giuseppe is chatting to Suzanne; a singular gleam flares up in his dark eyes, and he adds: "More reliable than those your friend wanted to recruit himself in Kaba."

I've understood. He too suspects that Giuseppe had an understanding with the four cameleers, first to leave us and then to gratify us with a mock attack

He too I've just written and I don't even know whether I've already formulated my own conviction on that point, a conviction that hasn't yet crystallized into absolute certainty.

Yes, it seems evident now that Giuseppe has had recourse to extreme means and has truly taken risks, with a disputable honesty, with the goal of intimidating us and forcing us to turn back, renouncing the accomplishment of the task that Gilberte and I have imposed on ourselves.

Why has he done that?

In what interest has he incessantly played a double role of appearing to approve of our search for Antonio, and even participating in it, while surreptitiously multiplying the obstacles in our path, attempting to paralyze our essential means of action?

That might be very grave, but cannot be entirely so. In any case, there is every chance that we shall soon know what we're dealing with, the confusion being forcibly clarified as soon as we reach our goal.

He is pretty, the fifteen-year-old Arab, our guide, whose father now introduces him to us, and he mounts a black thoroughbred which would not be unworthy of the stables of a billionaire. He has bouffant blue culottes, a braided pink jacket and an immaculate turban around his smooth mat forehead, the face of a medallion devoid of a patina, in which the nose is detached with finesse from the streak of kohl of the eyebrows, under which the eyes of a gazelle live and palpitate.

"He's an utter darling," declares Suzanne, frankly, "and since I no longer have a cavalier, I'll attach myself to his person until the end of the journey. What's his name?"

"Ben Taleb," replies the child, who understands French, although he scarcely speaks any foreign language except his father's jargon.

But Giuseppe has just approached, with a circumstantial face, for farewells that are very cheerful.

"Let's hope," jokes Suzanne, "that we'll meet again in a better desert."

Gilberte straightens up, bracing herself with an amused smile, as if a burden has just been removed from her shoulders. A sensation of deliverance fills us both simultaneously, so precise and so powerful that we discern the reflection of it in our gazes, which intersect.

Flax has found a mean to extract himself from Giuseppe's adieux. At the moment when the latter calls him, we perceive him ferreting along the bushes on the first steps of the mountain, and he has resumed the appearance of a hunting dog that we remarked in him at the beginning, when we first engaged on the desert trail.

Now the ascension commences, after a thousand sweeping bows exchanged with Mohammed and the notables of his tribe. There is nothing disagreeable about it, because, for the moment, we are still under the cover of green oaks, turpentine trees and carobs. The oblique light glides gently through the foliage; a strong and intoxicating odor rises from all the saps that are fermenting in the ground or circulating in the trees.

But already the vegetation, the grasses, brambles, mosses, thickets and stands of trees are all thinning out; the chalk is augmenting underfoot, and then sandstone, and soon it is bare porphyry rock that is invading the landscape everywhere.

Here, at least, as Suzanne observes, the marble-cutters have not passed. We have, in fact gone around the foot of the ridge of the aerial sculptures, and the zigzag road only has one objective, to attain the highest pass of the massif of the foothills, in order to reach the other slope.

An hour later we reach that culminating point, and we then enjoy a vision that will remain in the memories of all of us: to the north, the calcined chaplet of mountain slopes that rise toward the Palestine along the Arabah; to the west, three concentric saddlebacks of white summits, a pullulation, a chaos of peaks, needles, impossible geometric forms carved by some demented lapidary, and beyond—for that frozen ocean is the mountainous hinterland at the foot of which Spalatrina lurks—the wing-beat of the immensity, the infinity of the sky and the sea, joining up, a sky and a sea of indigo: the Mediterranean; to the south, finally, the profound rip of the Arabah: a colorless furrow that goes to join, at the limit of vision, the desert plains of Arabia and Egypt.

We begin to descend again in a series of zigzags stiffer than those of the ascent, and we fall upon an intermediate plateau, or rather a bowl, in which the fantasies of the troglodyte marble-cutters reappear, here and there, ruined by the ages or by plutonian cataclysms.

Then the ascent commences again, and ends on a ledge that winds around an arid cone. Another rise, and suddenly, at a turning of the zigzag, we emerge n to a vast aerial terrace, from which massive towers launch forth, the shored-up cupolas of a restored château dating from the crusades. That is the Institute.

An avenue planted with unknown trees leads to the enclosing wall, which extends over all the accidents of the little rocky plateau. Gilberte and I stop and we look at one another without saying a word, gripped by an identical emotion. Behind those livid walls lies the secret on which our imminent destiny depends.

Rapidly, we confer. As it has been decided that I will present myself to Harward alone, as a negotiator, I confide my horse to Ben Taleb, while Gilberte and Suzanne strive to retain Flax, who is yapping fully.

The bell of the guard pavilion awakes singular echoes in that solitude, and as it is doubtless rarely agitated its appeal is immediate followed but an effect. An old Arab in a caftan appears and looks at me curiously. I hand him my card. He disappears, and a rather long time goes by.

He finally comes back and invites me in good French to follow him. We traverse a dense and low vault, and then corridors with loopholes in which a delightful coolness reigns. They lead us to a large vestibule, as high as a nave, the ogival bays of which refract and filter the solar spectrum.

A few steps, and here we are in a sort of oratory furnished in the Oriental style. A silken door-curtain opens and a man clad in a long blouse comes toward me, extending his hands, gloved in fine white cloth. It's Harward. His welcome is more than warm.

"This is bold and very French; the prophet has decided to go to the mountain, which, in your case, is complicated by the most tedious desert in Arabia. Yes, you have deranged Arabia Petraea in order to see me anyway. It's a great honor for me...an honor that I scarcely merit, after my involuntarily discourteous attitude in Spalatrina."

Once more I remain nonplussed before the cordiality of the man, around whom Giuseppe strove to accumulate the blackest suspicions. The vague grievances with which he had labored our ears incessantly, and with the aid of which he had silhouetted a fantastic Harward, a vain Chinese shadow of the man whose frank and harmonious voice put me so much at ease at that moment, melt away at a stroke and for ever. I respond as best I can.

"If I've deranged your desert, it has turned the tables by playing me all sorts of dirty tricks. The last one consisted of a Bedouin fantasia, of which my companions and I consider ourselves fortunate to have been unharmed spectators, although, according to all appearances, we were to have been its victims. For I'm not alone..."

Harward did not let me finish.

"What! You've been the victim of aggression? No, but that's comical...excuse me, I'll explain. I had read the most frightful things about the Bedouin marauders of the El Tih desert. Then, when I arrived here, I bought the entire tribe of the Allaouin, the only one that counts in this region. It cooperated in the construction of the edifice and assures my portage today, and, in general, all my provisions. Yes, the Allaouin are my market gardeners, and my suppliers of meat. In addition, they police the desert, for my account and at my expense. Well, by their own confession, they do not remember having cognizance of any event of the kind you describe."

"That's exactly what their sheikh told me."

"Oh! You've seen him? You know him?"

"It's him who served as our guide as far as the oasis where his people camp."

"Then it's even more implausible...but patience, we'll get to the bottom of it, and the guilty parties will be punished, I'll answer for that."

"Pooh! It's not worth the trouble. I mention it to you simply to justify the request for hospitality that I've come to address to you...for my two companions, at least."

"Never mind! You have no need of justification...those ladies and you are at home here, and you can stay as long as you please. With that, let's not make them wait any longer."

He took me to the guard pavilion with a jovial and almost juvenile haste, wanting to do the honors himself to the two young women. While silhouetting them in a few words by way of introduction, I went pale with confusion at the thought of the duplicities with which I was enveloping that gallant man, the lies with which I was responding to his simple and confident frankness.

Gilberte, in accordance with our recent agreements, became a demoiselle Couturier, who was simply a friend of Suzanne Saint-Marceau. It was futile to disguise the identity of the latter, for evidently, he was going to recognize immediately the little crackpot that he had sent away in Spalatrina, and might even suppose that we were making use of her in order to set a trap for him.

In any case, there is no means of deadening the shock because of the urgency he is bringing to his welcome. Come on! It's necessary to speak.

"Let me...dear Master...warn you that one of the demoiselles is the daughter of the celebrated writer Saint-Marceau. She is coming contrite and repentant..."

Once again he cuts short my speech, not without a fugitive pallor bringing out the bistre halo around his bright eyes.

"I knew that...I learned of her departure by wireless, but I did not know in what company she was attempting the difficult journey...at present, all is for the best."

The portal is open. Harward positively escapes me. His haste frightens the picturesque group formed by Gilberte and Suzanne, whose juxtaposed knees are serving as a pedestal for a heraldic Flax, quartered with *gules.*

A momentary hesitation, a correct inclination before Gilberte, and Harward approaches Suzanne with his hands extended

"I have been delighted to learn from Monsieur d'Autremont that you have returned to sentiments more compatible with the happy and legitimate insouciance of your age..."

Confused, Suzanne searches for a response, while Flax extends a condescending paw toward the scientist, which makes us all burst out laughing. The ice is broken. At an order from Harward to the porter, Arabs come running and take charge of our mounts. Ben Taleb makes his finest salaam to the scientist, who invites him to refresh himself, but he refuses; he wants to return to the douar before midday, in order to reassure his father regarding the accomplishment of the mission that he confided to him.

I slip a gold coin to the bold child. Gilberte shakes his hands. Suzanne kisses him brazenly. He departs delighted, and somewhat overwhelmed, I think, in spite of his ethnic phlegm, by the two blue eyes that are studying him inexorably...

XVIII

The rooms indicated to us are very simple but everything there is ordered in accordance with a severe hygiene that does not exclude comfort: furniture of sandalwood and cedar, bed with copper columns, bare walls painted with ripolin, one entire face of which is a glazed bay from which the view plunges over the Arabah. Every room has a bathroom in which ten taps each emit a different kind of water: sulfurous, gaseous, calcareous, mineral, etc.

At midday the bell invites us to lunch set up under an awning in the open air. Harward presides over it with the cordial and charming simplicity that is decidedly a trait of his character. It embarrasses Gilberte and me, and we multiply the false smiles for fear that he might perceive our constraint.

But he sees nothing, being too occupied in documenting us on the fashion in which he composes and varies his menus, for which he has procured Spalatrinan entrecote, fillet of Arabic roe deer, grillade of Syrian wild boar and the terrible shallot sauce that accompanies a certain refrigerated turbot...

"Refrigerated is meant elliptically," he explains, "for it simply means that it's conserved by procedures of intense cold."

"You've thrown one, Master, with your explanations," quips Suzanne, who has a mania for wordplay.[12]

---

[12] The wordplay does not translate well; Suzanne is employing Harward's use of the word "elliptically" to justify her joking reference to him "throwing a curve-ball."

And with regard to intense cold, do you know what my friend Maud Doppendale, the daughter of one of your...victims told me?"

Harward has stopped eating. He considers the enfant terrible with a surprise in which there is a hint of embarrassment.

"What do you mean, one of my victims?"

"But yes...since he's in treatment in your house."

This time a malicious smile creases the scientist's lips.

"Oh, that's right...I remember that Doppendale has, in fact, disappeared from Spalatrina, mysteriously, and that he let everyone believe that he was leaving for a cure in my house..."

"Well?"

The scientist's eye sparkles with humor. "Well, if you swear to me, beautiful child, that the secret I'm going to confide to you will die with you, and as late as possible..."

Suzanne extends her hand above the turbot.

"On the frozen entrails of this doubtless prehistoric fish."

"Good; you should know, then, that Doppendale is simply in Cairo, where he is, it appears, finishing a very scholarly study of the origin of feminine choreography in Egypt."

Suzanne, who thinks she has understood, blushes and snorts: "I'll tell his daughter."

"You've sworn..."

"That's true. Pardon me! All the same, men!"

"And now, know that I've renounced treating anyone at all here. Poor Cattledown was the last, or the penultimate, of my clients." He turns to Gilberte and me. "When one thinks, you see, of all the accidents that menace human life, of everything that complicates it, poisons it, devastates it or suppresses it prematurely, of all the deaths due to hazard or the play of natural forces, or which are caused by the work of the malignity and perversion of men…when one thinks about all that, one no longer has the courage to slow down anyone's old age, and one even doubts that one has the right to advise the adventure of a long-term treatment to anyone…above all when the outcome remains very uncertain."

The sudden air of lassitude spread in Harward's features is aggravated by a quaver in his somber voice and the chagrined mist that hides his gaze from us.

Gilberte is very pale and I divine that she is making superhuman efforts not to deliver her secret. But my own gaze begs her not to speak, to remain patient, to wait until a flash of enlightenment illuminates the question with which we are struggling entirely.

In fact, Harward has offered to show me the establishment, from top to bottom, while the young women take their siesta. If that visit reveals nothing sensational, if no suspect indication forbids us to have entire confidence in this man, then it will be time to throw away the masks and present him with our apologies in exchange for his explanations.

"The establishment," Harward tells me, as we commence our tour, "is divided into three sections: therapeutics, physics and chemistry. We'll commence with the last."

And there are rooms almost entirely glazed, in which the play of curtains permits the distribution or the interception at will of light. We file past serried ranks of test-tubes, flasks and vats, some of which are retrenched behind hermetically sealed grilles. Harward gives me explanations devoid of interest for a profane individual like me.

The physics section retains me more. I have the usage explained of a host of measuring instruments the like of which I have never seen.

"Thanks to this apparatus, slightly forbidding in aspect or, on the contrary, of puerile appearance—for here is an esthesiometer that resembles a child's toy—I can now measure with a mathematical precision all the variations of the sensibility of a man, and not only his physical sensibility but his mental sensibility. And here is an electric keyboard that produces variations in sounds of different pitches, so that a patient sitting on this stool, and who is subject to a series of successive emotions. translates those emotions into a modulated and rhythmic song, sometimes with the most unexpected cadences."

"The secret music of dolor or pleasure."

"Precisely—and can you imagine that the instrument reveals to us not only that certain excessive states of soul are all dissonance, but it has permitted me to formulate a rigorous law: the same emotions determine absolutely identical reactions in individuals of the same temperament. Look, here's a graphophone that has registered the modulations collected by the electric keyboard in the course of an experiment in terror to which two young Arabs presenting the same physiological indications were subjected. Listen to the first."

The instrument produces a strange nasal chant with chromatic intervals, almost continuously ascending; it terminates with a kind of shrill organ stop from which the sound falls back abruptly to the initial fundamental.

"Now listen to the second."

And it is, in fact, an absolutely identical chant, with the sole difference that after the organ stop, instead of falling abruptly, the sound descends again via unequal intervals.

"It's marvelous," I say, "for even if one sets aside the comparative studies that it permits, a instrument that expresses phonetically all the emotions of the human soul is summoned, in my opinion, to fill a formidable lacuna in the art of musical composition, especially that which is applied to translating human passions into music. Don't you think that it ought to be put in the hands of all our young composers of opera?"

Harward smiles indulgently. "Unfortunately, the model you have before your eyes is unique; I spent two years constructing it and perfecting it. Lord Cattledown was very fond of it, as was another of my invalids, the last in date, a man still young attained by profound neurasthenia, delirious in form, who spent hours at this keyboard in order, he said, to hear his swan song—which is to say, the song of the last days that remained to him to live, for he believed that his death was imminent."

Abruptly, I am seized by an inexpressible anguish; I'm convinced that it's a matter of Antonio. My eyes riveted to those of the scientist. I ask, in an indifferent tone: "Is he still alive?"

"Yes"

But Harward has lowered his head as if to flee my gaze, and his "yes" seems to me to be tinted with an unanalyzable emotion. I am on the point of formulating a new question, but he does not give me the time, intimating with a gesture that I should follow him.

We go down a few steps and traverse a basement in which I detect the traces of ancient Roman vaults. After forty meters we come back up in order to climb thereafter an elegant perron that leads us to the doors of a vast pavilion with retreating wings: the section of therapeutics ad physiotherapy.

My attention is unfortunately too sparse and my nerves too taut for me to interest myself in Harward's technical explanations as he enables me to pass in review the various rooms respectively affected to blood transfusion, animal grafts, anesthesia, etc...the laboratories in which culture broths, poisons, animal or human ferments are simmering or dangerous liquefied gases are stagnating, the amphitheater of dissection, the areas devoted to radioscopy, electrotherapy, heliotherapy and thermotherapy—all the new branches of medical science that are only beginning to substitute a real science for the confused ensemble of empirical practices constituting the medicine of old.

Finally, two buildings galvanize my curiosity again: the wireless post and a factory for the production of liquid air. In the later, Harward limits himself to drawing my attention to the greatly reduced apparatus the serves to obtain liquid air almost immediately, by means of falls in pressure from two hundred atmospheres to sixteen:[13] a motor, two pumps and coils protected against thermic radiation, and that is all.

"What purpose does the liquid air serve?" I ask.

Then—a strange thing by which I remain seized—Harward is troubled, hesitates, and finally replies: "None. I hardly manufacture it any longer. It once served for special cures that I've renounced definitively."

"The treatment of old age, doubtless?"

This time he goes pale and looks at me askance. "Yes," he says, laconically.

---

[13] It is profoundly unclear how a fall in pressure could contribute to the liquefaction of atmospheric gases.

And as the visit is terminated, he takes me into a vast garden where trees and plants of all climates are growing.

"For we have here," he explains, "night and day, an almost constant temperature between twenty-five and thirty degrees for nine months of the year.

Traces of emotion still alter his voice and his gestures remain feverish. What living enigma is this man, then, and what has he done with Antonio? Tomorrow, if no new fact appears, I shall release the dogs.

With that, I think that I have forgotten Flax, and that the moment has me to utilize his marvelous sense of smell. In any case, we shall know from him whether Antonio's trail stops at the threshold of the Institute.

I make the remark to Harward, a trifle insidiously, that his establishment only has one fault: it constitutes, in my eyes at least, a frightful solitude, for, apart from the Arab servants and two or three laboratory assistants that we have encountered, lost in the emptiness of immense rooms, it seems devoid of all humanity.

"I have, in fact, let go of my former staff, and who knows, I might perhaps close the establishment itself in a few weeks, for it has ceased to respond to the new orientation of my research and labors."

The voice, firm again, has not hesitated this time. Harward seems somewhat relieved by the unexpected news that he is announcing. His facial expression is that of a captive who has suddenly remembered that the hour of release is imminent.

"I'll quit you now," he says, with his benevolent smile, which has reappeared. "for I have a formidable correspondence to put in clear and no stenographer. You must be in need of rest yourself. There are delightful hammocks here, under that clump of oleanders and olives, and beyond them an admirably rhythmic little waterfall whose natural song combats the most stubborn insomnias. Take advantage of it until this evening.

Well, no; I shan't go to sleep; even if I wanted to, I couldn't. A multiple presentiment, somewhat hallucinating, but which I can't qualify or define with precision, is racking my brain, doubling with palpitations the beating of my heart.

Something tragic is in the air. Harward has gone pale and become disturbed at the precise points where I foresaw that he would go pale and become disturbed. Once again, what has he done with Antonio? Exactly what part did he play in his disappearance? Is Antonio still in the establishment? Why would he have remained here? Is he dead or alive?

All those questions are whirling in my head and their frantic round is spreading more shadow than light. I can't deduce anything or divine anything; I don't know anything, but I want to know, and I shall.

And it is at the moment when I tacitly affirm my henceforth unshakable determination to know that a muffled prolonged howl nails me to the spot. I have recognized the voice of Flax, and I am immobilized, straining every fiber of my being in order to determine the direction from which the sound is coming.

There, behind the arbor of the hammocks, in the hollow of a fissure whose upper projection forms the top of the soporific waterfall, a stairway plunges and disappears among the foundation-stones, the ancient Roman substructures of the terrace. Flax's voice is coming from that poorly-lit orifice. I launch myself forward. A tiled pathway, the debris, one might think, of an ancient round-path, espouses the folds of the rock and leads to a stairway, passing under the projection to

147

which the entry of daylight is blocked by the vertical sheet of the waterfall; there are sites even more profound in the Swiss gorges.

Flax's voice is nearer; he is howling mortally. Hesitating at the entrance to the stairway I whistle softly and almost immediately I hear his disordered, stumbling bounds climbing the steps, very awkwardly, because of the darkness.

"Let's see, Flax, what is it?"

A flickering gleam dances in the depths of his eyes, normally so calm. He extends his neck toward me in an expression of invitation and supplication, forages my hand with any icy nose and grips the bottom of my jacket with his teeth. He wants me to follow him. Broad and beautifully curved, all in pure granite, the stairway turns in an endless spiral, and is soon completely dark. Fortunately, I have on my person the small electric lamp that is part of the classic apparatus of the tourist-explorer.

The decent continues and seems unlikely to end soon. I have the impression that we are plunging into the entrails of the mountain.

Finally, the stairway ceases turning; disposed in a perron, five or six steps conclude on a narrow landing. No opening or issue is visible.

Flax crawls along one of the walls, whining, then flattens himself and stretches himself, his nose against the ground, and recommences his lugubrious anthem, while scratching the rock with a gesture of digging.

I examine the wall, and then the paving-stones, of the little landing. It's implausible that a stairway of such importance doesn't lead anywhere; thus, the narrow cellar in which we find ourselves must open in one fashion or another. Perhaps a trap-door is framed in the paving-stones, or one of the symmetrical blocks of the wall pivots on itself under the action of a powerful spring, at some secret command.

But I palpate, sound and ausculate the exiguous stone décor in vain, inspecting the slightest crack and the cement joints, but can find nothing. I am scarcely skillful in that sort of research, however; it would require the hyperphysical vision and extranatural flair of the famous Sherlock Holmes, and I have neither the cloth of a policeman nor the vocation.

I confide my discouragement to Flax, having acquired the habit, during the great storm that passed over my life, of talking to him as if to a person. He was then a baby of thirteen months, a candid and gentle baby, as frank as all impulsive creatures, but also a virile baby, haunted by all the appetites of a man; for dogs are, mentally, only failed humans.

"Come on, Flax, that's enough; we have nothing more to do here, and in any case, your whining might betray us. Yes, it's understood that you ask no more than to obey, on condition that we don't stray too far from the trail you think you've found, and by means of which, by a mysterious olfactory suggestion, you associate the sepulchral taste with the odor of Antonio's cravat. So be it then; we'll explore this rocky cliff from top to bottom, all the way to the slightest creases, and if the mysterious cellar of which we can't find the entrance—although it must exist, I'm as sure as you are—has any other exit, it will have to deliver its secret to us. All right?"

Flax acquiesces with his head, his fine head of a domesticated wolf, but the resigned furrow that stripes his hirsute forehead expresses a vague disapproval, or perhaps simply the annoyance of obeying, of giving in, when he is sure that he is right.

XIX

For a good hour Flax and I have been searching the fissures of the little rocky promontory that supports the terrace of the Institute, all the niches and all the excavations that cosmic forces, the muted work of subterranean waters, or simply the usury of time have hollowed out there, some of which were subsequently utilized by Nabataean stone-cutters.

I have left a word at the Institute for the young women, in order to have full latitude to prolong my absence without awakening anxiety, above all without alarming Gilberte.

We have gone down dirty gray bare slopes, up and down again, sometimes salt gray, sometimes clay gray and sometimes smoked gypsum. Now we are at the foot of the ridge, in a narrow treeless curve where nothing seems to be alive: no plant, insect or animal of any kind. A funereal silence reigns here, the silence that must have weighed upon the world in the earliest times of its genesis. What a contrast with the cheerful plateau up above! Why does the valley seem to have been particularly harshly treated by Providence?

It's true. I remember now that an Arab tradition situates in this place one of numerous Sodoms of which there is mention in early writings—which is to say, of some city that was once destroyed by the fire of Heaven. And, in fact, an odor of sulfur trailing at the bottom of this little gorge evokes the cuisine of Hell, of which it must once have serves as a crucible in the time when the cradle of the world played the role of a fuse-wire in the short-circuits of celestial anger.

A brief bark on the part of Flax, followed by a hoarse growl, which is a threat, or at least a comminatory warning—addressed to whom?

We are at the entrance of a grotto, whose frame, this time, presents traces of sepulchers, volutes, capitals, garlands trophies etc. There is even a vestige of a frieze of triglyphs, the ornaments of which seem to have been passed through the soot of a chimney.

It is, no doubt about it, an ancient hypogeum transformed subsequently into a abode for Jewish prophets, and I now understand Flax's nervousness.

There is something more painful to see than a tomb, and that is an empty tomb; there is something even more painful than an empty tomb, which is a tomb from which the living have expelled the dead, and where the usurpers have left nothing in their turn but the traces of their profanation: alternate generations of the dead and the living succeeding one another in the same caverns, sheltering in the same darkness, as if there were not enough room for the living in the sunlight, on the free surface of the globe!

While I meditate thus, like a man prodigal with his time, Flax has disappeared into the interior of the mausoleum; but he is already coming back, his tail aloft, his nostrils quivering and a triumphant gleam in his eyes.

Evidently, he has made a find. Furthermore, he is manifestly inviting me to follow him, and I do not have to be begged. The daylight diminishes and we advance toward the depths of the grotto, and I'm obliged to have recourse to my lamp, because I've just bumped into something that has started to groan dully.

Flax stops, but without giving voice, proof that there is no immediate danger. The luminous beam sweeps the chalky soil. A man is lying there, rolled up in a double black burnoose, who offers all the appearances of a Bedouin.

He wakes up entirely, blinking like a nocturnal bird surprised in its lair, and looks at Flax and me with a strange expression of resigned lassitude. The face, intelligent and criss-crossed by very fine wrinkles, is that of a man of about sixty, European in type beneath the sunburn that has cooked him thoroughly. The bright eyes, cracks like those of old Breton mariners, are alive, with an indefinable, moving life, in the strange ascetic face, the lower part of which is eaten way by a vast gray beard.

The man has sat up and is staring at me with an ardent and sympathetic curiosity.

"You're welcome, Monsieur," he says to me finally, in very good French. And, without giving me time to respond: "I'm not the Bedouin you might have thought; I'm a Frenchman, a Parisian, like you, no doubt, but a Parisian who has been wandering for twenty-five or thirty years—I don't know exactly how many—in this land of mourning and silence, this land of shadows from which life withdrew centuries ago. I've come here to meditate, to dream, and also to carry out research that impassions me...

"Like the majority of tourists or rich pilgrims who push as far as this region, you must have hired a dragoman in Kaba or Kerak. Ask him about the 'Frensaouf' of the Arabah...they all know me...and he'll tell you that I'm harmless and that even the Bedouins of the desert respect me. Perhaps he'll also tell you that I'm a little mad"—an embarrassed, constrained smile creases his lips—"but no matter. Throughout the ages, sages have passed for madmen, haven't they...?

"I told you," the old man went on, that I've been in the country for twenty-five or thirty years, and I believe that I'm not much mistaken, even though certain bleak days and certain heavy nights have seemed like years...oh, if you knew, Monsieur...if you knew how I sometimes miss Paris...Paris, where there were walls between my slumber and the nocturnal life of the rest of creation...hold on, I didn't dare ask you this immediately, but it's been such a long time since I've seen anyone from out there, will you talk to me a little about Paris? Only a few words..."—a childlike supplication enlivened his blue gaze—"tell me about the enormity of its noise, its feverish and quivering life, the street and its drama, changing at every minute, the streaming of the boulevards, the people running madly after omnibuses, especially the incessant, lugubrious tread, like a fusillade, of horses' hooves, their uninterrupted rattle of murderous salvos...oh yes, murderous, the poor beasts know something about that..."

Although slightly disconcerted I nodded my head approvingly at the old man's ramblings. Was it necessary to correct him, to tell him about the recent upheavals in Paris, to tell him that the torrent of life no longer only flows on the surface of the Parisian soil but in its subterranean veins, that the crackling salvo of horses' hooves is no longer anything but an image relegated to the oubliettes of ancient rhetoric?

What would be the point? Better to maintain him in his error, to celebrate the only Paris that he has known and loved...and that is what I did.

His gaze, suddenly passionate, radiated such joy as I revived on my lips the obsolete Paris of old, he drank with such ardor everything abolished, everything overturned, that I poured out for him, that it would have been cruel to open his eyes.

I extended my hand to him without a shadow of irony.

"Wait," he said, "I owe a great joy to you; you've faithfully revived before my eyes the Paris that I shall probably never see again. Let me testify my gratitude to you in my fashion—which is to say, in the measure of my humble means. You love antiquity, I can see that—which is to say, the life of old, of the time when this desert country, which is, alas, no more than the sepulcher of the civilization of which it was the cradle, was pullulating with men made in our image. Well, I'll enable you to put your finger on that epoch; I'll do better than that, I'll show you one of those men of old, yes, a man of flesh and bone, asleep for four thousand years, intact, almost uncorrupted, in a superb sarcophagus, a double envelope of metal and glass. It would be a pretty gift to make to the Louvre for someone who had the means to ensure its transport there."

"You're doubtless talking about a mummy."

"You're free to give it that name...for me it's a man, like us, and I take pleasure, from time to time, in deciphering his history in his admirably conserved features, in the unaltered form of his body...but come, follow me, you'll see that I'm not exaggerating."

My curiosity, I admit, was white hot. We went out of the crypt. Sketchy steps climbed along a nearby buttress, which I recognized as forming part of the foundations of the Institute. The old ascetic went up the stairway at an alert and rhythmic pace, preceded by Flax, who, nose to the ground, sniffing and ferreting, gave a false appearance of guiding us.

The climb seemed to me to be rude, and when the old man finally stopped outside the collapsed entrance to a hypogeum, the place appeared to me to be too highly perched for an ancient sepulcher of some importance, not to mention that it seemed improbable that a mummy of distinction—as the man had said—had been able to escape the scientific missions and the host of archeologists who, over the centuries, had explored the region methodically. And would not Harward have signaled the singularity to me himself?

While we penetrated cautiously into the partly-collapsed vestibule of the cellar, the old man said to me, as if responding to my mute doubts: "No one in the world can have any knowledge of my find, and you'll see why..."

I relit my lamp, by which he was amazed, like a child.

"What a marvelous invention that is! If we had know that in my time! I make use of a torch, but the smoke suffocates me, and it spoils the spectacle...now, watch your step, for..."

A stifled howl from Flax cut off his speech.

The artificial corridor we were following ended in two steps leading into a quadrangular redoubt without an exit, exactly similar to the one that I had discovered at the bottom of the spiral staircase.

"An ancient burial chamber," the old man commented, in the hushed voice that one adopts in churches.

At the same time, with a gesture, he drew my attention to Flax's furious scratching, while extended on the ground, which he only ceased to claw in order to sniff one of the joints in the tiling.

"A companion like that would have spared me a month of long and difficult research—for that's precisely what preserves my find against any profanation; this chamber is, properly speaking, only a interior vestibule of the hypogeum situated below it, which communicates with it by a stairway of six high steps. It's necessary first, therefore, to divine the existence of the invisible stairway, and then to discover the secret that brings it to light and permits access to it, That double solution cost me about a month of laborious perseverance, but when one leads an existence like mine one isn't miserly with one's time. One idles, one muses around the task undertaken, and one eventually ends up attaining one's goal.

"When, from the fact that this vestibule had no reason for being unless it communicated with a veritable burial chamber similar to others I had seen elsewhere, I concluded that such a chamber must exist, I never ceased trying to discover the means of penetrating into it. First I sounded the walls, then the vault, and finally the paving stones, for it was in the last place that the idea of a second story came to me. Listen to this."

He leaned over the place where Flax was continuing to snuffle and scratch and struck the flagstone with the flat end of a pickax that he had picked up a moment before in a corner of the room. It rendered a hollow sound.

"That's all," he said, "but it took a month to think of it, and then another month to find the secret that commands the pivoting of the stone. It's simple, though as you'll see."

He introduced the spike of the pick-ax into the juncture, at a place where the seal of the cement presented an unobtrusive gap. I heard the sound of a click; the rectangular flagstone pivoted on its longer axis and fell back on the first step of the stairway that appeared. Flax immediately plunged into it and disappeared into the darkness.

Shortly afterwards, I heard him whining, the sound of which seemed to be coming from the bottom of a well.

The corridor at which the steps ended did, in fact, offer a rather steep slope. It rose up again thereafter to form a new vestibule. I was surprised to see that the vestibule in question was separated from the chamber in which the prestigious mummy lay by a thick partition wall, apparently intercepting all communication between the two cellars. Perhaps I would not even have suspected the second if the old man had not suddenly showed me a depression in the form of a navel in the exact center of the partition wall.

As he had done before he introduced the spike of the pick-ax into the depression, and one of the blocks in the wall pivoted on itself. At the same time, it appeared to me that an intense cold fell upon my shoulders.

"Child's play," he explained, "the command of the spring being too visible."

The funerary chamber into which we finally penetrated was a profound and low-ceilinged room, so deep that I could scarcely make out the extremity of it; only Flax's voice guided me, while the hermit, familiar with the place, advanced deliberately. He seemed insensible to the glacial cold piercing the open wall, which increased progressively, as if it were emanating from the depths of the room.

Suddenly, a metallic gleam shone under the beam of the lamp, and an indescribable emotion nailed me to the spot.

I had before me, posed in an arcosolium, something that the old illuminate had mistaken for a sarcophagus of the epoch of the pharaohs. Imagine a giant shell, of the normal dimension of a coffin, a coffin with cylindrical sides, presenting the mat gleam of polished cast iron.

There was a large oval opening in its median part covered with an operculum screwed on the body of the cylinder. The man started unscrewing that operculum slowly, while marveling at the respectful attitude of Flax, who was lying down, his head between his paws, at the foot of the coffin, and moaning softly. When the operation was concluded, he lifted out the enormous screw with metallic reflections, and withdrew it, not without difficulty.

An opening appeared, permitting the gaze to plunge into the interior of the cylinder. It was protected by a convex lenticular disk, the material of which was a dense crystal, or, at least, a substance having the appearance of glass, transparent and as limpid as diamond.

The old man invited me to project the beam of my lamp into it and look.

I obeyed, and what I saw initially transfixed me with fear.

Immersed in a diaphanous liquid that filled the shell to capacity, an almost naked body lay supine, arms folded, hands joined, the head almost touching the conical summit of the shell. And it was not the bound, bandaged, tarred head of a mummy but the admirably conserved body—living, one might have thought—of a contemporary individual, whose features I could not distinguish very clearly because of the disposition of the ocular, which confused visual rays that were too oblique.

When, leaning over at the appropriate angel, I was finally able to examine the face at leisure, a terrible emotion, and then a increasing horror, ran through my veins. The electric lamp shook in my hands, agitated by a convulsive tremor, and I could hear the disordered beats of my heat against the wall of my chest.

The face was that of Antonio Banchi.

It was also covered, like the limbs and the entire body, by a thin tissue, which one might have thought coasted by a substance that was fluorescent in places. That mask of sorts did not prevent me from identifying with certainty the face that it molded, for it reproduced faithfully the features of which my memory had retained a precise imprint, thanks to the numerous photographs of Antonio that I had been shown.

Eyes closed and lips sealed, the effigy resuscitated him in an even more striking fashion that of a small terra cotta bust placed on the mantelpiece in the Banchis' drawing room, the delicate modeling of which I had often admired. But the artist had at least been able to insufflate his work with a flame of life, while the rigidity of the mask that I had before my eyes, its absolute, definitive immobility, was that of death.

For a few minutes, at least, I remained mute, inert, incapable of disentangling the horrifying, contradictory fables that my imagination was already weaving around the somber and hideous mystery. The voice of the madman—for decidedly, only a demented reason could have assimilated that contemporary corpse, conserved in I know not what aseptic and incorruptible liquid, to an Egyptian relic—brought me back to myself.

"You see, even the hair, which the deceased wore long and curly, has not been subject to the slightest alteration. Let anyone tell us after that that our methods of embalming are superior to those of the ancient Egyptians!"

The hermit might have rambled on in that fashion for a long time if, suddenly penetrated by the terrible gravity of my discovery, I had not felt a need to finish with it, and get out of that tragic subterrain as soon as possible, to inform Gilberte and discuss with her the means to employ in order finally to make Harward talk. I was, in any case, chilled to the marrow by the terrible cold that reigned, which only the old man continued not to perceive.

"I thank you," I said, respecting his illusions, "for having initiated me into this beautiful find. It might have a great archeological and ethnographic importance. The Louvre, undoubtedly...that's an idea, and I'll think about it. In the meantime, if I can be useful to you in any way...if you have need of money for your repatriation...?"

He shook his head, a bitter smile stretching the fatigued crease of his mouth, but without the face losing its serenity.

"I thank you in my turn, but inasmuch as money would be no use to me here, except to get me robbed..."

I almost had to use force to get Flax away from that strange coffin, in which reposed the remains of an individual whose living odor he had learned, over long days, to discern, and perhaps to love.

XX

Dusk was falling rapidly when I reached the doors of the Institute.

A feminine silhouette raced toward me, supple and wiry; it was Suzanne. Breathlessly, she spoke:

"Finally, there you are; I was beginning to be afraid. Can you imagine that I'm all alone...that I've spent the afternoon all alone...it's unimaginable isn't it? No, worse than that, its intolerable, and you're going to swear to me that we're going to leave for Kaba tomorrow, as early as possible. I have my claque at the Institut, as Papa said when, blackballed by the Académie des Moral Sciences, he was advised to persist in his candidature."

"But what about Gilberte?"

"Oh, yes, let's talk about Gilberte...I haven't seen the tip of her nose all afternoon...or rather, I saw her for just two seconds, as she came out of the library...and that was to tell me that she had a terrible headache, that she was shutting herself in her room...that she might not have dinner...and that she begged you, when you returned, not to worry about her..."

I was astounded, not because a sudden indisposition on Gilberte's part could be reckoned implausible, but because her desire that I shouldn't worry about her, when she was suffering, as she must be, since she said so, contrasted so strongly with the tender solicitude that marked our quotidian relations, especially since the departure from Kaba, that I had no doubt that something grave had happened.

"That's nice isn't it?" Suzanne went on—but I was no longer listening.

"Flax," I said to the dog, who was making a fuss of the young woman, "follow me."

And I headed swiftly for the colonnaded gallery where our rooms opened.

"Scratch at your mistress' door," I commanded him.

He did not have to be begged, the word "mistress" having recently developed in him a sort of sixth sense, of which he was hastening to enlarge the domain, like a dog for whom the caresses of a woman had a new and rare softness.

Lending an ear, I heard a rustle of paper, and then Gilberte's voice, distant and utterly changed: "Who's there?"

"It's me, Gilberte…excuse me I'm very anxious."

"Don't be alarmed my friend…I am, in fact, suffering a little, and if I dine I'll dine in my room."

"In that case, I'll send you the professor…"

"No, no, I beg you; I have no need of anyone's care."

An impression of ill-contained fear has altered the timbre of her voice. Great God, what's happening?

She adds: "We'll see one another tomorrow, in the morning."

This time I am no longer master of myself. A cry escapes me. "Gilberte, you're hiding something from me. I sense it; I'm sure of it…your voice is utterly changed…it's necessary that I see you right away…in any case, I have excessively grave news to tell you."

"Me too, and it's for that reason, and that alone, that I'm asking you, that I'm begging you, to let me collect myself, at least for one night…tomorrow morning, you'll know everything…and we'll decide…together…"

162

"So be it, Gilberte…you're right to remind me that I have no right over you…less than any other, that of imposing my presence and my advice on you when you judge it inopportune."

Only a stifled sob responded to those bitter words. What should I do?

That whispered dialogue through a closed door could not decently continue. Already, Suzanne, whom I had asked to wait for me at the end of the gallery, was approaching, impatiently. Some stranger might be watching…the electricity was illuminated everywhere.

A bell rang, and then three strokes of a gong resonated from the direction of the central pavilion: the signal for dinner.

I shivered at the prospect of finding myself, for at least an hour, face to face with Harward. No, no, the idea of seeing that man now, of talking to him tranquilly about indifferent things, while the specter of Antonio loomed up between us, was insupportable to me. Why, in any case, should I sit down at table, since I was sure in advance of not touching any food. My decision was made.

To Suzanne, who arrived, I said: "You're going to report me ill, Suzanne—which is to say, to give my apologies to Harward. I won't be dining this evening."

"What, you as well!"

"Yes, but in my case, it's understandable. I've scaled all the peaks in the vicinity, and I'm exhausted. Excuse me yourself."

Young Saint-Marceau shrugged her shoulders and stuck her tongue out at me.

"You're a swine, so there, to leave me alone with that ogre Harward…and simply out of amorous spite."

"You won't be alone, I'll leave you Flax. See that he doesn't lack anything...in exchange, he'll watch over you."

She menaced me with her finger. "You'll pay me back for this...!" And she disappeared.

The night went by, mortal and interminable, heavy with all the grim silence that weighs upon Asiatic solitudes, a night of agony such as I hope never to live again. Incapable of going to bed, much less of sleeping, I had gone down into the garden, where the moon was trailing her white veil over all those unfamiliar vegetables, some of which were grimacing and fantastic under the silvery ash. It disappeared and everything around me was black.

Every time my footsteps approached the waterfall that hid the superior entrance to the crypt where Antonio was asleep, a frisson ran from the nape of my neck to my heels. Whence came the intense cold that reigned around the metallic vat containing his remains? What could be the nature of the liquid that bathed the unfortunate's body...so miraculously preserved that the idea of applying the word cadaver to it did not even occur to me?

And why did the abnormal bier that contained the body have the entirely characteristic form of those cylinders with conical summits that serve as receptacles for gas compressed at high pressure?

Why, above all, had that singular coffin been fitted with a glazed opening permitting the surveillance of phenomena susceptible of occurring inside?

Why, finally had those who placed the body there, and protected by a undiscoverable secret the modern entrance to the crypt, not acted in the same way for the ancient issue, still intact with its infantile mechanisms, with which the sagacity of a semi-madman had reckoned so easily?

Meanwhile, my gaze did not lose sight for a single instant of Gilberte's wide open and illuminated window, which I perceived from far away, in the arch of an arcade, a luminous eye open in the depths of an orbit of darkness.

What was she doing? What could she be doing? No shadow, at any moment, appeared in the vast area of the window. Gilberte, in consequence, was not delivering herself to any movement, as not budging from the place where she was sitting? What occupation or what dolorous dreams were absorbing her to that point? Was she reading? Was she thinking? How could she maintain such immobility for hours?

In the end, I wanted to clarify the matter and gently, muffling the creak of my soles on the gravel or the sandstone flagstones, I slid very close to the window.

And again, I heard at intervals the sound of moving paper that had struck me at the moment when I came to negotiate at her door.

She's reading! Is that possible? Can one shut oneself away in order to spend an entire night reading, without explanation, without remorse, without any concern for the mortal anxiety into which one is plunging the person who loves you?

Fortunately, here comes the dawn, which chases away specters, abolishes the aerial tragedies of fever, and pours the hope of eternal resurrection over the earth. And here comes Gilberte herself, who has perceived me at her window and is coming toward me, for it seems that emotion has cut off my legs.

That is because the mere sight of her face has put death in my soul. She has been weeping, she is still weeping, long, scintillating tears, droplets of sunlight, one might think, springing one by one from the mourning black of the pupils. My approach, naturally, precipitates the crisis. She abandons one of her hands to me and, her head buried in the hollow of my shoulder, burst into silent sobs, the heart-rending shocks of which make her frail and charming body tremble against me.

"Gilberte," I say to her, infinitely more emotional than I would like to appear, "talk to me, tell me right away what's wrong. You mustn't, you can't, exclude me from your chagrins, and besides, I'd rather die…far from you, yes, die miserably, no matter where, rather than spent another night like this one."

Gilberte has raised her head, and gazes for a long time, with eyes of languor and lips of suffering…the tremulous lips of children who have not finished weeping. And I no longer perceive anything but her charm of a flower still quivering from the storm that has passed over it, the exalted iris odor of her skin and her hair.

Finally, she says: "Go back to your room. You'll find in the drawer of the small table a manuscript with broken seals, which I've just put in there. Read it, as I've just done myself, then we'll decide immediately what it's appropriate to do."

"But who gave it to you?"

"I took it…stole it, if you wish. Harward, who thinks I'm fond of stories of voyages, told me that his library was full of rare and curious works about the Syrian coast, and that I'd find enough there to occupy me for a few good hours. While I was rummaging everywhere, you know with what objective, a shelf that made a tour of the room at the height of the upper floor attracted my attention by virtue of the slightly baroque bindings. It was a false shelf only composed of the spines of books, which dissimulated a sort of cupboard, in which a few not-very-voluminous files were scattered. No key closed the cupboard, nor was the false shelf defended by any secret, Harward being the only person to go into that library. One of the files bore, at the head of the papers contained by the same string, a large sealed envelope with the inscription: *For Gilberte Riviez-Banchi, after my death.*

"As I had recognized Antonio's handwriting, I had not the slightest hesitation. I took the envelope and went to shut myself in my room, pretexting a headache, as you know. The manuscript it contained, I read and reread all night long. You're going to read it in your turn; then, urgently, we'll make a decision as to what to tell Giuseppe, in whom I no longer have any confidence. Go, my friend, I'll wait for you, and know that I remain with you in thought. Yes, remember that whatever might happen, whatever sanction events and our duty reserve for that double reading, remember that I love you and that I have sworn an oath to love you for as long as I live."

"That alone counts for me," I affirmed.

And I was so overwhelmed that I quit her, completely forgetting to tell her about my own discovery, which was certainly more important than hers.

XXI

This is Antonio's manuscript, the lamentable confession of a man who, under the exterior of a businessman, remained a sensitive dreamer, an unfortunate invalid at odds since adolescence with the mysterious disease of *black ideas*, which is as old as humanity, although it changes its name in accordance with epochs and languages.

These pages take us back several years. As they are classified in the order in which they were written, and cut up into chapters, there is no difficulty in reconstituting the approximate dates. To those who might smile at the redundancies, and the pathetic adjurations that drew so many tears from Gilberte, I will simply recall that, being Italian, Antonio shares the gifts of exalted sentimentality of his race.

My dear Gilberte,

First of all, excuse my style, reminding you of the efforts I have made to assimilate your language.

In any case, I do not know whether I shall have the courage to give you, later, these pages to read, which I am writing day by day and in which I am burying, it seems to me, in small fragments, what remains to me of youth.

Perhaps I have never been young, or at least have never perceived that I was, which comes to the same thing. I have always been waiting for something that ought to come, something more perfect, better, definitive, a culminating state of all my physical and mental strength—and the years have passed thus, and when I looked back, I perceived that it was my youth that I had spent in that apprehension, that I had doled out like a rosary of doubt and anguish, without knowing it, in the expectation of something else.

And that something else has come in its turn, and it is old age. Perhaps it was even upon me for a long time before I was conscious of it.

It was, above, all, on the day that I loved you, Gilberte, that I understood that I was old...irremediably. I was thirty-two, with wrinkles in the corners of my eyes, my temples streaked with silver, my hamstrings soft, my lips twisted and hollowed out, as if by a perpetual nausea. Already worn out by affairs, I drank ether in order to stimulate myself, like so many others.

I felt old, I tell you, and if your sixteen springs enchanted me, plunged me into ecstasy purely by virtue of their splendor, they also frightened me, terrified me like a magic spell, a trap especially designed for individuals of my species. Yes, your sixteen years made me afraid, afraid and ashamed, me who had not known youth.

A day came, however, when I was emboldened. You had been clement, you had been kind enough to admit that a man like me could aspire to spend his life at your knees. And you had permitted me to open my heart to you.

Finally I obtained from you the authorization to ask for your hand from those who had adopted you and who also took the place of a mother and father for me. That was yesterday. And yesterday has become today. You know their objections, the reasons in the name of which they are constraining me to wait. I have been obliged to incline before those reasons, and we are now in accord...but if they knew, and if you knew!

Wait! Love! Are they not two mutually exclusive verbs? How can one stand up to the odious tortures of waiting when one is in love? How can one love if the center of gravity of the soul only remains in equilibrium thanks to the lead mortal to all passion that is called resignation—the resignation that, alone, permits waiting?

Now, you know, Gilberte, that I love you. By that I mean that it is impossible for me to conceive of the future without you. You can think what you like; I'm stating a fact that I don't take responsibility for excusing or explaining. There is an irresistible pressure of my entire being toward you, an impetus such that I can see no other possible bifurcation at present than death. And that word "death," which returns to my pen for the second time, indicates well enough the distress in which I have been living since you have so deliberately adhered to the adjournment decreed by your parents.

Perhaps I'm simply neurasthenic, like so many others, but my God, to what degree! I need silence and obscurity, a perpetual silence and obscurity. By night I live a different life, infinitely superior to that of the day. My senses are duplicated, and refined, my nerves blossom like the supernatural and supersensible flowers that they are. Then I hear the mysterious language of things, of all the things that surround me, to which the darkness renders their mute life, so deplorably oppressed by light and noise.

Oh, I would like to be dead already, in order to the reintegrated with the womb of things, to dissolve to them, to live their life of brute matter, the only eternal one.

I've consulted Professor Harward of the Chicago Academy of Medicine, one of the great scientific names of America. His reputation is as solid on that terrain as on that of general biology.

He has made me understand that he believes me to be suffering from depression rather than illness, but that he has no pretention, at first sight, or even at second sight, to form an opinion on my condition.

For he posits this in principle: out of twenty maladies, there are at least nineteen for which it is impossible to place a sure, absolute diagnosis. And then, what is a diagnosis? An application of the method of induction, an antiscientific, antiexperimental procedure that consists of concluding the particular from the general.

"Yes," he said to me, "you can recognize the classified symptoms of the disease, the local troubles that it determines, but the disease itself, the direct or atavistic heredities that are its profound roots, the five or six generalizations that will have connected the virus with their flaws, their infirmities, their passions, you will never know; even less will you know the remedy to apply, the fashion in which it is necessary to comport oneself in the presence of all those algebraic Xs. In any case, there is no 'remedy,' and there never has been."

That is the consultation that one of the great scholars of America gave me on the subject of my malady.

Would you believe it, Gilberte? His simple and sober word, the authority of his voice, ardent with conviction and sincerity had, in spite of everything, given me so much confidence that I returned to see him. This time, he consented to ausculate me, to sound me out, and this was his sentence:

"Your arteries have a tendency to harden, and the nervous centers are reacting poorly. You're drinking too much ether. Stop drinking it, progressively, and you'll be cured."

Oh, if I could follow his advice! But I can't...it's beyond my strength. I can see your start from here, Gilberte, your reproving gaze...forgive me. The truth is that I only owe the faculty of breathing, feeling, thinking or sleeping to a constant saturation with ether. The harmony of all my intellectual and physical functions is at that price. It's also the only odor that I can tolerate; it neutralizes all the others and creates a sort of atmosphere for me that permits me to brave all the human and animal odors by which I'd otherwise be positively asphyxiated in no time, so subtle is my sense of smell. The odor of life, the moldy odor of time gone by, the seed of decomposition deposited in the depths of every second that passes...the rotten breath of the hour lived...pooh!

Expelled from the cadres of university education for crimes of opinion, Professor Harward had disappeared from Chicago several months ago, without his disciples and pupils, or even his most intimate friends, knowing exactly what had become of him. In elevated scientific circles it was affirmed, however, not without some irony, that the master was pursuing abroad sensational experiments susceptible of revolutionizing medicine and biology, or at least modifying completely their prudent and routine orientation

Le Journal of Paris brought me today precise new concerning those experiments, attributed by its English correspondent to Dr. William Thager.[14]

---

[14] Author's reference: "*Le Journal* 28 August 1913 (first page)." The reference is slightly mistaken, but the article cited is real and accurately reproduced, in slightly abridged form; it actually appeared on the first page of *Le Journal* on 30 August

I reproduce here in full the article from the Parisian newspaper.

Liquid Air Conserves Latent Life

We have received news from England of veritably extraordinary experiments that have been carried out at John Hopkins Hospital in London.

They tend to prove that life and the vital functions can literally be suspended for a rather long time and then made to reappear without risk and without inconvenience.

These experiments have been made by Dr. William Thager and his pupils.

Animals—lizards, reptiles or rays—were placed in special bottles into which liquid air was introduced. It is known that liquid air produces a considerable lowering of temperature. In the present case that lowering was more than a hundred degrees below zero. In order that death would not occur abruptly, a current of oxygen was sent into the flasks until the cooling was complete. The persons who conducted these trials could only handle the containers with special gloves in order to protect them from the intense cold, which would have burned them.

The animals rapidly took on the appearance of cadavers and became absolutely rigid. They were then abandoned for a month.

1913. However, there was no John Hopkins (or Johns Hopkins) Hospital in London at the time, and the name William Thager appears to be fictitious, so the article seems to have been a hoax. The reference does, however, suggest a contemporary setting for the story, at odds with earlier implications.

They did not receive either nourishment or air naturally. No exhalation of carbon dioxide was observed, nor any movement; in brief, the most scrupulous examination could not reveal any trace of life.

At the end of that time the animals were taken to a warm bath and taken out of their flasks. To the amazement of the witnesses, after a light massage, they returned to life perfectly.

A hen's egg on the point of hatching was placed in the same conditions. Four weeks later, it was taken out and broken. The chick that it contained was perfectly alive!

This morning, the New York *Herald* reproduced the article from the Parisian newspaper and added this:

Might the name of William Thager be a pseudonym adopted by Professor Harward, who, before his departure from Chicago, had proposed the project of undertaking analogous experiments?

At any rate, we have it from a reliable source that our compatriot has created an Institute with this goal on the Syrian coast, in which he is pursuing strictly parallel research, and that he counts on extending it from animals to humans.

He is, it seems, even seeking volunteers courageous enough to brave the risks of the suspension of life by immersion in liquid air, the least of which is that the resurrection of the patient appears to us, at least, to be terribly problematic.

Advice to amateurs desirous of savoring the pleasures of latent life in a sealed jar in a liquid at a hundred degrees below zero.

I have made enquiries regarding the article in the *Herald*, which I took at first to be simple American humbug. It was not a matter of a hoax. The biological and physiotherapeutic Institute created by Harward has existed for more than a year. It is situated in the mountains of Spalatrina, that very recent Syrian Cannes, about whose vertiginous rise you know. A member of the Club of Undesirables, which has an affiliate out there, had given me rigorously checked news.

Harward has made his first human experiments. They have all succeeded beyond his hopes. The Turkish government had delivered him three men condemned to death, who were promised that their lives would be spared if they submitted voluntarily to the proof of immersion in liquid air for a duration to be determined with their approval.

The first was left immersed for four weeks, the send for three months, and the third for six months. In the three cases, the resurrection—or, rather, the revivification—was carried out gradually as soon as the bodies were transported into the decongelation vats. They were restored safe and sound to normal life, but it appeared that the temperament of the last—a sickly degenerate—had benefited from the absolute repose of the organism, and that his physical and mental health were manifestly ameliorated.

All of that left me pensive…and the more I thought about it, the more it seemed to me that Harward's discovery was the equivalent of an elixir of longevity. Yes, it is almost to assure people of immortality to be able to extinguish and reignite the flame that is consuming them at will, to suspend the course of their poor human existence, relieving them for months or years of the burden that will appear to them to be lightened of all the weight of the time they have not borne.

And it is also a suppression of old age, or at least an adjournment of it.

Oh, how I aspire to that absolute repose, that plunge into annihilation, into total unconsciousness.

Two months have gone by, bringing me the capital, culminating disappointment, which I sensed in the air.

A further delay has been imposed upon me, perhaps of four or five years, and you, my adored Gilberte, have once again ratified the decision of my uncle and aunt. It appears that you consider yourself to be too young to confront marriage.

Too young! Oh, the lie of words, and how I would love to be too young, having never known veritable youth! No, but it is to die of it, to think that perhaps I too was young, at some turning of my life, but that I never perceived it, that I never had a clear consciousness of it, and that the days, the months and the years passed by, only bringing me the perpetual sentiment of growing older.

I have just learned that one of the founders of Spalatrina, Lord Cattledown, a friend of our former club president, in residence for three years in Chicago, is going to depart again for Spalatrina and solicit from Harward the favor of a suspension of life of several years. Perhaps it is a fantastic rumor. I shall find out this evening what is behind it.

Lord Cattledown has confirmed to me from his own mouth his formal intention to submit to the antisenility treatment, as he calls it, for several consecutive years.

"However," I observed to him, "What will you gain by that dangerous game? When you come out of the experimental chamber, you will resume life, your life, at the point where you left it."

"Yes, in other terms, that is called taking a step back in order to jump better. But is it not already something in to be able to put off the final jump by a few years? And then, frankly"—his eyes suddenly gleamed with a quasi-ferocious malice—"it will be a rude joy for me to find myself caught up in age by the comrades who presently treat me as a blockhead and a graybeard because they're four or five years younger than me, and that will be a joy such that the worst risks wouldn't be paying too dear for it."

"Your reasoning is perfect," I told him, finally, delighted to see that lord, universally esteemed by his peers, a man heaped with age and all the favors of life bitten by the same chimera as me, "and I approve all the more sincerely because I'm ready to follow your example. Will you render me the service, right away, of proposing my candidature as a long-term patient—let's say five years—to Harward, who knows me."

Lord Cattledown acquiesced, and a month after his departure, he cabled me the following response:

Harward refuses formally to adhere to your proposition. He shrugged his shoulders when I transmitted it. "At his age! The fellow must be mad, as he had a slight air of being when he came to consult me in Chicago."

Mad! Perhaps I am, without knowing it, without anyone knowing it. How do I know? Can we ever know that we have all our reason? You alone could judge me, Gilberte, if I had the courage to open to you what is inside me...the inferno that I carry within me, of which you could so easily make a paradise...

I am drunk with joy.

For months I spun out words miserably in ink. And now, a dawn of hope, of boundless felicity, is rising in the confines of my being, and everything is illuminated, everything is resplendent, even this poor piece of paper, which is suddenly dazzling me with its virgin whiteness, having been so lamentably gray and dull while I was pouring the mourning of my life on to it.

I have flexed Harward. He consents to my delivering myself, for four or five years, from the horrors of waiting, from the burden of existence, from the torture of twisting incessantly in my heart the red-hot iron of a hope that might never be realized.

Those long years during which I must still wait for you, and which would make me an old man, I am going to pass in absolute unconsciousness, in the forgetfulness of my frozen organs, similar to those polar animals in which life finishes at the end of the boreal summer, only to be reborn with the resurrection of the sun.

If that resurrection does not take place for me, at least I will not know it, and I will have slipped without suffering, without even suspecting it, from apparent and relative annihilation into absolute annihilation

That is, I believe, the most beautiful death for which a human can wish.

The supreme proofs that Harward felt obliged to impose on me are reaching their conclusion. He has tried in vain to arouse my suspicion against science and against scientists of his species, to exalt the benefits of precarious normal life such as nature dispenses, to show me the gulf that exists between a simple laboratory experiment and the crazy attempt that I persist in making in the wake of Lord Cattledown, of whom nothing proves at present the possibility of revivification, to enlighten me in a general manner regarding the dangerous folly implicit in the fact of risking death in order to escape a few temporary annoyances, when life still promises long years of compensatory joys—in sum, to repeat incessantly all the contraindications, for me, of an adventure scarcely excusable in an old man desirous of screening himself from the biological laws that weigh upon his age. He finally had to yield before my inflexible will.

We have exchanged on that subject, and with regard to the formalities by which Harward thinks he ought to cover his responsibility, several encrypted letters, a precaution exaggerated by him in order to avoid any possible leak, any indiscretion susceptible of intoxicating, as he puts it, another brain than mine, of inciting anyone else to follow my example, having decided himself to stop there with regard to long-term human experiments.

Furthermore, I have had to swear to him solemnly and on my honor the most absolute secrecy.

Spalatrina...the last days.

The rather long voyage from Louisville to Spalatrina has not shaken my resolution, as Harward hoped. The hard moment was that of the departure from the railway station, the rupture with quotidian life, habits, familiar faces—a rupture of which I alone can savor the bitterness.

Then the movement of the train definitively dispersed any mollifying image, except yours, since it carried me toward the accomplishment of our dream, the dream that ought to bring us together extemporally.

I have left a few words back there for you: the necessarily mysterious farewell that circumstances impose on me, plus a commercial testament that will put all my affairs temporarily in the care of Giuseppe. I have sounded out the prodigal child recently; he appears to me to be perfectly capable today of playing to his honor the important role that the prolongation of my disappearance will gradually impose on him.

This Harward is a prodigious man! He has come to fetch me here in an airplane in order to spare me the desert crossing. When I expressed my astonishment that, at his age, he practices a sport that appears, at first sight, to be incompatible with the withdrawal, the contention and the mental calm required for the manipulation of the great problems of intellect and science, he said:

"Bah! A truly modern man ought to develop all his faculties, including those that exteriorize and multiply his emprise over things as well as those that only enrich him subjectively. In any case, I have French blood via my father, and France is, as you know, the cradle of great aviators, and also the greatest number of aviators; they're even found, I'm told, among the old men conscripted to the Senate."

In any case, Harward conducted the airplane that served us as a vehicle with a marvelous manual surety, and a coolness that would have forced my confidence if I had not given it to him without reserve a long time ago.

The last moments have arrived. My papers are secure in Harward's library, and will soon by joined there by this manuscript dedicated to you alone.

It appears that my temporary sarcophagus—if I dare put it thus—will be a glass receptacle with a double wall protected against all radiation by a preliminary silvering of the external wall, which will give it the appearance of a metallic coffin, and a vacuum will be created between the two. The envelope is moreover, equipped with a kind of crystal ocular closed by a similarly silvered glass operculum.

I wanted to see all that with my own eyes, but Harward, who is wrongly suspicious of my impressionability, refused energetically.

The supreme moment has come, and that is the only one that is really anguishing, but it will be brief. I shall be put to sleep by means of a light narcotic; then my entire body, including the face, will be coated with a chemical composition destined to protect me from the mortal burns of the cold. Then, finally, I will be deposited in the layer of liquid air at a hundred degrees below zero.

Harward is here. He has told me to stop writing; his bright eyes are fixed upon me, in which I read a sincere emotion, a profound pity...

You also, my adored Gilberte, will give an emotional memory to the man who loved you, naively but strongly enough not to be able to support the idea of living for so many years far from you in space and time...in time, especially, in the pitiless fight of which he dreamed of suspending, at risks and perils, the course of his own days.

XXII

For some time I after had finished reading, my forehead remained riveted to my palms, my eyes wandering over the gaps between the lines without seeing anything, entirely given to the deadly and tragic vision that rose up within me.

Antonio, the poor passionate dreamer whose pure and rare heroism I admired in spite of everything, the Don Quixote who had dared to measure himself against annihilation, was not dead! One could not be sure, certainly, that he was alive, but he was no longer disappeared nor deceased, as Gilberte and I had ended up supposing. He figured once again in the world, not only in the social world but in the little world, previously inviolable, that Gilberte and I were to one another. And if, materially, he occupied a very tiny place in the former, his moral place in the latter was immense, preponderant, ineradicable in a way, by reason of the rights conferred upon him by the antiquity and nobility of his martyrdom, and, alas, Gilberte's platonic promises.

While I am still crushed under the weight of that extreme conclusion, someone knocks gently on my door.

It's Gilberte who comes in. She is still very pale, and I know not what tragic anxiety fixes her charming features while she tries to read my own distressed face.

"Well? You've read it? You've finished reading it?"

Let's go! It's necessary that nothing prevents us from seeing the situation in its true light and making the decision that is imposed.

"I've done more than read it, my dear Gilberte; I've seen Antonio."

"Safe!"

Oh, the lovely and noble movement of that cry of joy, emotional and frank, because it is uttered by the compassionate friend, by whom the fiancée, whose heart belongs to me in spite of everything, is momentarily eclipsed. Immediately afterwards, her eyelids flutter dolorously under the reaction to the shock of the new proofs implied for Antonio, as for us, by the hypothesis of his resurrection.

"Nature will soon pronounce, I hope, for, according to the dates of the manuscript, the experiment is reaching its terminus, and perhaps we have a right to demand of Harward its immediate cessation. If I told you that I've seen Antonio, it's only in the apparatus in which he is sleeping his strange apparent death, which might, perhaps, alas be a definitive death, and..."

Gilberte opens her eyes wide, dilated by horror.

"You've seen that?"

"Yes. I discovered by chance, yesterday, the inferior orifice of the ancient funerary crypt in which Harward has deposited the immersed body, apparently in order to preserve it from eventual profanations. The place was, in any case, poorly chosen, for the secret has fallen into the hands of a sort of hermit, a Frenchman whose reason has been obscured by a personal catastrophe, and who proposed to me yesterday sending his find—to which he attributes a pharaonic origin—to the Louvre."

Gilberte does not reply. She reflects profoundly, her gaze lost, a charm of distress at her temples, two stray tears amid the mourning fringes of her eyelashes.

Then, finally, in a form voice nuanced with tenderness, the inflections of which are no longer troubled by any languor, she proposes:

"We are betrothed, Georges, and I have given you forever, as you know, all of my life to come. Whatever might happen, no foreign consideration can prevail in the balance in which our mutual happiness lies. But, faithful to my oath to you, I also intend to remain faithful to the duty that links me to those whose adoptive daughter I am. We have sworn to do the impossible in order to recover the man who was their favorite child, the hope and consolation of their old age. Since he has been found, we don't have the right to hesitate for a minute.

"Firstly, we ought now to play a frank game with regard to our host, for whom good faith and correction command respect in spite of everything. You will be my spokesman; you will tell him who I really am, and what we have come to do in his house, and you will ask him to suspend immediately the tragic experiment by virtue of which a man had been in a state of apparent death for several years.

"Antonio's morbid desire might have been formal and precise on that point, fixing an immutable delay, but above that there is the sane will of all those who love him and for whom the idea of the anticipated death, artificial as it is affirmed to be, is intolerable. I am sure that he will understand, and will comply, insofar as the agreed term of the experiment is so close to expiration."

"So be it, but"—and my voice trembled in formulating the terrible hypothesis—"what if Antonio, resuscitated, demands that you realize the dream in the expectation of which he plunged himself into annihilation?"

A singularly subtle gleam lit up in Gilberte's eyes. She said: "Antonio only knew the girl of sixteen that I was then. She has passed, as all the different beings that we are in the course of our lives pass, never to reappear. In five years I have become a woman, a woman whom Antonio will scarcely recognize, and whose sincere amity will console him for the loss of the other..."

"And Giuseppe?" I said, suddenly, with a twinge of malaise, almost of fear, in seeing the disturbing silhouette surge forth in the background of our accord, having forgotten him so completely.

"I believe that our duty is to inform him immediately," said Gilberte, loyally.

"However," I objected, not without embarrassment, "you said just now that you no longer have any confidence in him."

"Undoubtedly, because his suspicions and hesitations of an exaggeratedly skeptical man accorded poorly without nervousness, but he is, in spite of everything, Antonio's brother, his sole legal representative here. He has, moreover, associated himself with all our efforts; we cannot, in justice, omit consulting him at the moment when they are about to end."

"Consulting him?"

"Yes, I think, all things considered, that before requesting a conversation with Harward, it's necessary to inform Giuseppe of the discovery that you have made and to obtain, if only for form's sake, his assent to the energetic solution that is imposed."

"And the manuscript?"

"Let's not mention it, since it only concerns me."

"So be it. I'll do my best to join Giuseppe within twenty-four hours. As long as he doesn't have any idea at the back of his mind in the same vein as the one that was responsible for the attacks in the desert."

Gilberte made a gesture of resigned lassitude and I left her in order to investigate the means of putting myself in communication with Giuseppe as quickly as possible.

The Arab servant who was saddling my mare told me that I would encounter Allaouin porters half way to the douar, because it was the day of reprovisioning. I decided then to go on foot, in order to be able to follow rigorously the shorter path by which the porters would be climbing. One of them would doubtless consent to return immediately to the douar in order to ask Giuseppe to come to meet me, or to arrange a rendezvous on the mountain.

I was finished planning the details of the message, while descending the first projections of the abrupt slope along which the path snaked—a thin gray zigzag slightly dirtier than the rest of the ridge—when a sound of voices made me shudder in every fiber.

Perhaps because the atmosphere had an exceptional sonority, and perhaps also because of the great universal silence, the two voices that I heard seemed to be conversing a few paces away from me, and I discerned their slightest inflections, although the conversation was apparently taking place a hundred meters below the place where I was. I had immediately recognized the lightly shrill and nasal timbre of Giuseppe's voice, which was, in any case, pronouncing banalities scarcely interrupted by the yeses and noes of his interlocutor.

Why did I shudder? Simply because Giuseppe appeared to be conversing familiarly with a stranger in these mountains, which he had never visited before.

I descended as rapidly as the slope permitted, and soon perceived Giuseppe, who was, in fact, talking very familiarly with the old Parisian. Already, his eyes, surprisingly mobile under the heavy eyelids, were sounding the projection from which I emerged. He climbed up to meet me, his arms extended, overflowing with cordiality, all his Italian exuberance in his lips and his gestures.

"Ah, it's you, carissimo. I'm glad. I was just about to ask for a meeting via the porters. How are you? And Gilberte? And little Saint-Marceau? And Harward? There's news, eh? I can see that in your face..."

"Indeed, I..."

"Not here, not here, walls have ears...there are even more than ears than walls...as those of that old cenobite prove...see how he's watching us, the old mausoleum owl. I'll tell you his story in a little while..."

"I know it."

"Ah!"

And it seemed to me that Giuseppe repressed the start of a man who has just been stung by a horse-fly.

"All the more reason, then," he said, lowering his voice and also his eyes. "He's acquainted with everyone...he's loquacious, a braggart...but let's move on, he's about to draw nearer.

A sidelong glance assured me that the man had not budged. However, as our conversation was going to have an exceptional gravity, I followed Giuseppe, who drew me away.

XXIII

The impression produced on Giuseppe by the news I have brought him has been formidable, and that observation relieves me a little; it proves at least, that he did not know anything, that he was not the odious traitor whose appearance he took on for a few days in my imagination.

The profound amazement at the story of my discovery—a kind of bewilderment into which no simulation enters—and then his pallor and dejection when I submit Gilberte's expeditious decision to him, demonstrates fully that he was ignorant of all that we did not know, and that he was not expecting the imminence of the terrible blow that the solution of the experiment might reserve for all of us: a solution to which we are going to constrain Harward.

I respect the stunned mutism in which he is absorbed when I have finished speaking and I wait for him to speak.

"This is serious, very serious," he says, in the end, "and Harward is going to have terrible accounts to settle, for nothing proves that he didn't exercise suggestion on my poor brother to ensure himself of a subject—which is to say, one victim more."

I could have annihilated that malevolent hypothesis, which attests once again the irreducible hostility of Giuseppe toward Harward, by opposing Antonio's own confession, but I abstained from doing so, Gilberte not having authorized me to divulge the secret of the manuscript.

"I don't share, as you know, your suspicions in regard to Harward, but, all things being equal and whatever the degree of his moral responsibility, it will be necessary for him to incline and stop the experiment immediately when he finds himself in the presence of an order from the brother of the patient, the entitled legal representative of the Banchi family."

"Por Dio!" Giuseppe said, with a start. "Let's not commit that imprudence. Above all, let's not invoke the family—which is to say, right, the law, justice—let's not threaten, without absolute necessity, the man who, as you know, holds Antonio's life in his hands."

"But there's no question of a threat."

"Yes, yes... my intervention alone would have a comminatory character. Since we've sagely decided to leave him ignorant of my presence here, let's persist in that attitude...act without me...there'll still be time, in the case of failure..."

Undercut by a violent emotion, the words and phrases tumbled spasmodically, half-amputated, on the edges of his quivering lips.

"So be it," I said. "I'll take the step of finding Harward..."

"Not now, not right way, not today...it's necessary to anticipate everything. Harward might retrench himself behind a will written by my unfortunate brother, invoke a sort of mystical testament expressing his formal determination only to be returned to life on the date chosen by him...and in that case the torturer might secretly move the mortuary deposit in order to steal from us until the final day the body that we're reclaiming."

"What, then?" I said, shaken by the apparent logic of that argument.

Giuseppe reflected, a crease in his forehead, his eyes wandering in the void. Finally, he said:

"The fact of having placed his patient in that crypt, which only a miraculous hazard allowed you to penetrate, implies on Harward's part the evident intention to preserve him from all research. By revealing our discovery to him we'd be delivering ourselves, giving away our game; he'd conserve the possibility of opposing us, of making the body disappear at will. That's what it's necessary to avoid at all costs. What can we do? What can we do?"

He stopped, oppressed, moaning, a veritable distress in his eyes.

Suddenly: "I've got an idea. Tomorrow morning, early, you can act in regard to Harward without putting me in play, since I'm supposedly still in Europe—it's necessary not to show all our cards. In any case, the explicit will of Gilberte ought to be sufficient to persuade him, for she too represents the Banchis. Don't tell him, either, that you know where the body is...that would suggest the idea to him of removing it elsewhere, in order to conserve barriers against us."

"It's necessary, however, that I motivate my step, that I make him understand that I have absolute proof that Antonio is at the Institute."

"Imagine what you like...say that an indiscretion on the part of Lord Cattledown put you on the track, and if necessary, shelter behind Gilberte, who will remain in the wings…"

"And then?"

"Either Harward will yield, and all will be for the best, or, which is unfortunately more probable, he'll try to circumvent you, to gain time, of which he'll take advantage to put his patient in a safer place, and then he'll run into dispositions that I'll have had time to make, for my idea simply consists of recruiting a few reliable fellows from Mohammed's douar, who will guard the two issues of the crypt while I involve the commandant of the nearest Turkish fort in the affair."[15]

The plan wasn't bad, since it assured us of victory in any event. It offered the sole inconvenience of delaying a solution that my feverish Gilberte wanted to be immediate for some twenty-four hours. Doubtless I could have argued the inanity of so many precautions when the term fixed by Antonio himself for his proof was so imminent, removing from Harward any pretext for prolonging it against our will, but it would have been necessary to bring up the manuscript, the confession that, alone, informed us of that deadline, and once again, I was not authorized to do that.

At the most, I thought I ought to insinuate that we would gain time by choosing our Arab auxiliaries from among the porters, but Giuseppe, who said that he had thought of that, objected that they were unreliable wretches who would, in any case, he exhausted after their chore and would only be thinking about sleeping.

The result was, finally, that I approved his plan entirely, and we separated, arranging to meet the following morning at seven o'clock, the hour when I ought to be in possession of Harward's response, while Giuseppe would have made sure of all the dispositions agreed.

---

[15] This implies that the story cannot have a contemporary setting, since the last remnants of the Ottoman Empire had been obliterated completely by 1923, and strongly implies a setting prior to the Great War.

XXIV

Oh, the atrocious dream, or rather the nightmare, from which Gilberte and I are emerging, quivering with horror, steeped in sadness, devoid of the strength or will to foresee what tomorrow will bring...

She had adhered to Giuseppe's plan, although it appeared to her, as to me, puerile and superfluous, certain as we were that, once our masks had been courteously removed, Harward would feel obliged to yield to our insistence, no less courteously.

"We ought," she had repeated, "to incline before the will of Antonio's brother.

The day, in any case, was reaching its end, and the approaching night would not be long, although we foresaw the moderate agony that it would bring both of us; for if only a few hours of insomnia separated us from Antonio's resurrection, what an eternity of anguish the hours that followed would contain for us, when it would be necessary to disabuse the soul of the resuscitated, to initiate him gradually into the sentimental rigors of a Destiny whose eternal mobility he believed he had fixed, when he had only immobilized his poor personal life.

I knew that Harward started work at dawn. When the electric clocks of the Institute chimed six I presented myself at the threshold of his work-room.

His hand extended, an affable smile on his lips, he invited me to sit down and said that he was ready to listen to me.

And as his sharp gaze has already detected something unusual in my features, I want to spare him a perplexity that I imagine to be particularly cruel. As soon as

I sit down I come straight to the point: we have betrayed his hospitality; we are not simply the modest tourists whose roles we have played; only young Suzanne Saint-Marceau is playing her character naturally, ignorant of the real goal of our expedition; as for the pretended Mademoiselle Couturier, my fiancée, she bears in reality the double-barreled name of Riviez-Banchi, being the adoptive sister of Antonio Banchi.

And I remain stupefied, discountenanced, for the *coup de théâtre* that I expected is not produced. Impassively, Harward considers me with a sort of mocking bonhomie, waiting—I presume—for me to finish laying my cards on the table.

"How did you think," he finally said, "that you could put one over on an old psychologist like me? First of all, your story of brigands was unnatural"—in that, at least, the old psychologist was mistaken, as I told him later—"and then, the facility with which you accepted my precarious hospitality, your absence of any preoccupation with the length of your sojourn here, as if nothing and no one summoned you elsewhere, and you had no other objective in the word but contemplating the bald summits of the Djebel-el-Tih, had awakened my suspicions. An old newspaper band fallen from a valise, which bore the address of Mademoiselle Gilberte Riviez-Banchi, put me on the track of the truth,

"It only remained for me to wait for you to come—which is to say, to expect to receive from Mademoiselle Riviez-Banchi an ultimatum to which I would be obliged to yield. For, as with Lord Cattledown, it was only against my instinct that I consented to accept as a patient the poor man who hoped, thanks to the temporary death of his organs, to escape the apprehensions of I know not what sentimental crisis, of which he only ever spoke to me in covert terms."

Harward's explanations having given me confidence, and, only too glad to be able to repudiate prejudices that were not mine, I gave him a detailed account of the way I which I had discovered the crypt and succeeded in introducing myself into it. The scientist listened to me open-mouthed, his fists riveted to the arms of his chair, suffocated by astonishment.

"I should have suspected it!" he suddenly cried. "I should have suspected that the hypogeum, like so many others, had two issues—or, rather, that there were two hypogea there linked by a secret passage, as one finds in many mountain crypts. At the moment when grave reasons, which you shall know in due course, forced me to place the experimental container in the cellar where you saw it, I introduced it via the orifice of the cascade, the only known to me. I thought about sounding the back wall, but it rendered a normal sound, as did the paving stones, and I concluded that the secret of the cavern was safe, the closure of the orifice in question being almost inviolable. Furthermore, as I go down there every two days, sometimes every day, to assure myself of the perfect conservation of the body and replace the quantity of liquid air lost be evaporation..."

"The receptacle isn't hermetically sealed, then?"

"As you might imagine, because of the enormous tension of such a liquid, the conical summit of the cylinder has a circular opening, which is simply stopped with wadding, in such a fashion as to enable the interior compartment to communicate with the external air, white avoiding excessive evaporation. I counted, therefore, on my daily visits and the minute dispositions I had taken, to ensure my subject an inviolable repose. His condition, moreover, was excellent when I last visited him yesterday morning, and I hope that he has not suffered from your…incursion."

I affirmed to the scientist that my guide—whom he knew—had limited himself to unscrewing and replacing the lid of the ocular, without even touching the latter.

"He did well, for he would have been atrociously burned. In the meantime, your story proves to me that my dispositions were insufficient, and that is the first information that I have obtained from it."

He fixed me then with a kind of anxious curiosity, which nevertheless remained benevolent.

"The second will perhaps be furnished by the response that you make to the following question: how were you able to discover that Antonio Banchi had come to seek at the Harward Institute a remedy for a purely psychological malady, of which he might, in fact, only have been cured by annihilating his personality for a determined time?"

"I obtained it from Lord Cattledown," I replied, at hazard, remembering the falsehood that Giuseppe had suggested to me.

Abruptly, Harward's face darkened, assuming an expression of cold melancholy, from which all the sympathy that he had showed me thus far appeared to have been withdrawn.

He said: "I regret to inform you that your response is devoid of any plausible foundation, for Lord Cattledown was too much a gentleman to betray the oath that I demanded of him, and in any case—this is peremptory—he was in the course of treatment when I consented to yield to the already old entreaties of Antonio Banchi. Permit me to observe that my honest attitude toward a guest that I was authorized to treat as suspect cannot have vanquished his own suspicions."

The reproach went straight to my heart, at the same time as informing me that I had taken a false route in using duplicity toward such a frank man.

"You're right," I said, "and I offer you my most sincere apologies. I invented that small lie because I did not want to bring my fiancée into the matter. She was the one who found your name and your address on a packet of encrypted letters—which were, moreover, stolen by an unknown female thief. As for Lord Cattledown, I could not even attempt to interrogate him, for he was murdered a few hours after I manifested the intention of going to seek information from him."

Abruptly, Harward's hand weighed upon my arm in a spontaneous gesture that was almost supplicating.

"Wait, wait," he said, his eyes now seeming to follow in space the elements o a problem so arduous that his entire face was hollowed out and pale. Without looking at me, he said: "The letters, you say, were stolen by a woman. When did that happen and where?"

"In Candia, about six months ago, the first of May, according to Mademoiselle Gilberte, who remembers the date because the mysterious theft coincided with the departure of Giuseppe Banchi for America.

Harward shivered, but contented himself with clenching his fist a little more tightly on my arm. A rather long silence passed, and then, a suddenly fulgurant gleam appeared in this pale eyes, and he said to me abruptly: "Did Giuseppe Banchi know that you intended to interrogate Lord Cattledown?"

"Yes, he knew."

A new gleam, which one might have thought triumphant, illuminated the scientist's eyes.

"Good," he said. "And when you came to Spalatrina with your fiancée, Giuseppe Banchi accompanied you, and he knew that you were going to interview me at Gil d'Ax's famous soirée?"

"He knew that, and tried to dissuade me."

Harward stood up and paced back and forth, agitatedly; then, after a few moments, having recovered his impassive manner, he stood before me, and in a firm, resolute tone, tinted slightly by pity:

"I'm glad that your fiancée has not associated herself with your step; her presence would have embarrassed me. You're a man, and you're not attached to be Banchis by any direct link; you ought to know everything. Listen to this. Six months ago, instead of returning to America, after having stolen and deciphered as best he could the letters that you know, Giuseppe Banchi headed for Syria. He came to find me here, demanded and obtained to see his brother's body, and then expanded in cynical pleasantries, saying that that fashion of refrigeration was the idea of a lunatic and that I should refrain carefully from resuscitating the unfortunate madman, he and his relatives being only too glad to be rid of him so cheaply.

"I reproached him harshly for his attitude and his words. He apologized and appeared repentant, alleging that the situation that his brother had left in his hands was confused and terribly burdensome. That was, I discovered subsequently, the exact opposite of the truth, and that it was that situation, and doubtless the mirage of the large Banchi fortune, that pushed Giuseppe to wish for the definitive disappearance of his brother. He stayed for a few days, and one morning..."

For an instant, Harward's convulsive hand, his darkened gaze and the hoarse sound of his voice revealed an intense emotion.

"…I surprised him in the process of piercing the side wall of the container with a minuscule drill. Take note that if he had reached the second wall, the liquid air would have escaped immediately, and his brother would have been doomed.

"Immediately, I expelled the wretch, and, in order to make the patient secure from any further attempt, I placed the container in the crypt you know. I never saw Giuseppe again, but I'm almost sure…yes, sure…that it was him who murdered Lord Cattledown."

I started—which Harward doubtless attributed, not to a terrified disturbance whose cause he could not suspect, but to the dolorous emotion of a man on whom the indignity of a friend or relative has rebounded.

"For let me also tell you this," he went on, with the haste of an accuser intent on validating his assertions. "Giuseppe knew that you were going to attempt the impossible to recover Antonio, and had decided to block the route to the measure you intended. So, when, before the impossibility of making a murdered man talk, you wanted to interview me, do you know what he imagined?

"He sent me that evening, at the Libyan, at the hour when I was expected at Gil d'Ax's apartment, a veiled Arab woman, one of those houris ready for any task, who are easy to find in the indigenous quarter of Spalatrina. That woman told me—I'm translating her jargon—'One of my brothers who lives in the desert among the Allaouin, has just returned from out there; it's believed that the hiding place has been found where you deposited the body you know…return quickly, or all is lost.'

"Certainly, the news was grave, but tainted with such implausibility. I made the muslim woman understand that I suspected her of serving as the instrument of an impostor and threatened her with the authorities. She threatened me in her turn with her mountain brothers. Then, outraged, I said to her point-blank: 'And who knows whether you aren't the woman in the haïk who murdered the English lord?

"'And who knows,' she replied to me, tit for tat, 'whether you aren't involved yourself in that murder, committed on a dying man whose inevitable death would have injured your pride and your charlatanesque renown?'

"Shall I confess it to you? At that moment, struck by the change in the pitch of her voice, I had the clear impression that the woman in the haïk was Giuseppe himself. I had everything to fear from him. And as further entanglements with the law might really have retained me in Spalatrina long enough to favor some criminal attempt plotted out here, I left, limiting myself to sending my apologies to Gil d'Ax. What do you say now?"

Every one of Harward's revelations illuminated in my distant or recent memory one more ridge of a redoubtable edifice of irrefutable presumptions—what am I saying, overwhelming proofs—in which Giuseppe appeared as the most ignominious of criminals.

And suddenly, the thunderbolt of a crueler, more menacing evidence than all the rest gripped my throat. Giuseppe, the traitor, had abused me to the end. In continuing to play the comedy of suspicion, in asking me to postpone my step toward Harward under the pretext of ensuring the guard of the secret orifice, the existence of which I had so imprudently revealed to him, he had only been pursuing one goal: to remain master of the place for at least a few hours.

"It's only too evident," I said, completing my thought aloud, that he lied to me again."

"Who?" interjected Harward, in a blank voice.

"Giuseppe!"

"He's here, then?"

"In order better to dupe and betray us, he has accompanied us everywhere, except to your house, of course. But yesterday evening he was prowling on the mountain and I committed the folly of informing him of the discovery I had made and my intention to refer it to you. He asked me for a delay, pretexting the necessity of having the entrance to the cave watched in case of an attempted eviction on your part...you know his twisted loquacity. In brief, we arranged a meeting at seven o'clock this morning at the entrance to the crypt..."

I interrupted myself to take out my watch, but Harward was no longer listening to me; he had just bounded toward a chest of drawers; he took out two pairs of enormous gloves that one might have thought sculpted in chrome-plated copper.

He put one pair on, into which his arms disappeared all the way to the shoulders, and while I did likewise, on his order, he also provided himself with a powerful electric lamp. Then he said: "Come quickly...may it please God that we arrive in time."

The clock outside one of the laboratories only marked half past six, but a sinister presentiment gripped me.

We'll arrive too late, I repeated incessantly, for if Giuseppe had premeditated a criminal attempt, he would not have waited until the time when I was due to come in order to perpetrate it.

We ran to the cascade. At the bottom of the stone staircase Harward made me a sign to stop.

I listened, my nerves taut, and I thought I heard confused groans in a voice that was unknown to me.

Harward must have heard it, for he had become livid.

"Get ready," he said to me.

At the same time, his hand pushed a spring dissimulated in the cement of the paving stones. A trapdoor opened at my feet and immediately, through the opening that it unmasked, a whirlwind of white vapor sprang forth, enveloping us in its bitter and burning swirls.

"Too late!" murmured Harward, weakly,

The fuming cloud had no sooner cleared than we descended into the cellar, Harward in the lead, the beam of his lamp aimed in the direction from which the groans were coming, already enfeebled...

I shall never forget the horror of the spectacle that suddenly struck us.

Among the debris of the glass and stone with which the floor was strewn, three bodies lay, one of which was recognizable in its sculptural rigidity and pearl-gray mask; the second, Giuseppe, was also certainly inanimate, but still retained the flexibility that is like a delayed reflection of life lingering on the threshold of oblivion; the third, finally—the old Parisian—was writhing in the spasms of commencing death-throes. And all three were bathing in white, asphyxiating smoke, that one might have thought emanated not merely by the damp ground but from the bodies themselves, their garments, their skin and, principally, the various estuaries of the face: mouths, nostrils and ears.

"We've arrived five minutes too late," pronounced Harward, dejectedly. "Nevertheless go fetch help quickly—nurses, stretchers…in the meantime, I'll examine the wounded."

XXV

When the bodies had been taken upstairs, Giuseppe was dead, all the visible parts of the skin corroded frightfully, the face boiled and blistered, horrible to see. The old hermit was still alive, but frightfully burned, and his reason had finally given way under the shock.

Sad and dolorous work, accomplished by me under the whiplashes of a painful remorse, which were mingled with the chagrin of learning, hour by hour, that Harward's continuing efforts to reignite the flame of life in Antonio were not yielding any appreciable result. And Gilberte's tears were silent and as if retrospective, because they were flowing less for Harward's impersonal "patient" as for the mild exalted individual who had once loved her with such a noble and ideal passion.

This is an approximate reconstitution of what had happened in the crypt.

After our conversation, Giuseppe must have tried immediately to catch up with the hermit, to whom the wretch had assigned a role that reckoned his life cheap, but the old solitary had gone in another direction and Giuseppe only found him again at nightfall. He declared to him that he had reached an understanding with me to take delivery of the mummy destined for the Louvre, and offered him, in my name, a sum of money that the former colonel refused, not without astonishment, since he had already declined my offers, explaining to me the small value he placed on money.

As he had just made his dispositions for sleep and he judged the haste of my delegate inopportune, he advised him to come back at dawn, and did not want to yield in spite of Giuseppe's insistence—an insistence that would have appeared suspect to anyone but a poor illuminate, all the more suspect as one could not imagine that the removal and transport of a mummy could be effected without aides or appropriate equipment.

Giuseppe returned at sunrise and the hermit then decided to accompany him to the crypt and operate the controls permitted access to the cellar.

As soon as they were in the presence of the "sarcophagus" Giuseppe declared that he would commence by putting the mummy in a safe place, and asked the hermit to unscrew the lid under which he hoped, he said, to find the secret of opening the bier. The old man acceded to his desire, but, seized by a sudden presentiment, he thought of keeping watch on the actions of the stranger, who was then keeping strictly behind him. The lid, silvered on one of its faces, made a mirror just then; as he looked into it, the old man saw two hands ready to strangle him. Giuseppe's intention was evidently to attribute the responsibility for the criminal profanation he was about to commit, and which would leave Antonio plunged in definitive annihilation, to the old man, whose body he would leave at the foot of the arcosolium.

The old man just had time to turn round; Giuseppe's hands were already gripping his throat. But the hermit, built like an athlete, still very straight, supple and full of vigor thanks to his errant life, knocked his aggressor down with a punch full in the face, and then tried to immobilize his arms. It was then that Giuseppe, doubtless thinking himself lost, pretended to lose consciousness, and, having freed one of his arms, drew a revolver from his pocket and fired at the hermit.

The shot, going astray, struck the glass receptacle, which the bullet traversed with an abrupt furrow of fire.

The mass of liquid air was abruptly volatilized in a partial explosion, which shattered the walls of the receptacle. Intact, the "mummy" fell at the base of the fractured arcosolium, joining the other two bodies, which had collapsed one atop the other, carved by the glass, burned by the unvaporized liquid and asphyxiated by the white smoke that drowned everything...

XXVI

Gilberte and I are at the limit of our strength, neither one of us being born for tragedies. It is true that little Suzanne Saint-Marceau is scarcely better equipped for the mortal game of great upheavals of the soul, and yet she has supported them admirably

In any case, she only knows what we have wanted to tell her, and can only regret in Giuseppe the loss of a good comrade, a flirt who often amused himself with her innocently between two impostures.

Only we know everything, or almost everything. From the theft of the encrypted letters to the odious attempt in the hypogeum, we have reconstituted the entire criminal itinerary. A few lacunae remain, somber holes in which the sound hesitates, doubts that we prefer not to clarify.

What is the point, since we have the absolute conviction today that Giuseppe was capable of anything?

We have not waited for further protestations on the part of Mohammed to determine his innocence and his perfect honesty, recognizing the hand of the traitor in all the accidents and incidents destined to discourage us on the road or the desert.

But once again, we do not want to delve into all that, and there will never be any question of it between Gilberte and me. Let us say that it was a bad dream, what others call a nightmare.

Back there, there are two poor old people who are now mourning the loss of two young men in whom they had placed so many cherished illusions. And I think, not without bitterness, about the lies with which it will be necessary for us to support the fable of Antonio finally rediscovered, soothed, his appetite for life restored by us, and participating in a hunt in which he and his brother perished wretchedly at the bottom of a precipice.

Certainly, they will associate with that fable, in the same tears and the same regrets, the executioner and his victim, but we owe peace to the dead, to the innocent as to the guilty, because they both represent revolved expressions of humanity for whom nothing more is or can be.

Flax has understood all that, in his simplicity of soul, for he sat down with the same meditation—the same indifference, I was about to say—on the threshold of the two mortuary chambers. However, it is with a sort of relief that he is assisting in the packing of the valises that signifies that our departure is imminent—the departure that is a divorce, from the oppressive atmosphere of the Institute, which now has the effect on us of a vast laboratory of death.

For, as I have said, we are at the limit of our strength, and we have therefore seized the pretext of an alarmed radiotelegraph message from the Saint-Marceaus demanding their daughter, in order to hasten the final formalities that retain us here.

Harward will only stay at the Institute for a few more months, the time to liquidate everything, and to ensure the transport of his collections and scientific instruments. Then he will return to Spalatrina.

"Between now and then," he said to us, in a firm voice, "the mourning of the Banchis will have ended, and you'll be married…and happy, as I wish with all my heart."

THE MANNEQUIN

Researching an unsolved problem in electric dynamism (Carlier, the distinguished scientist, told us) I went to ground for a few months at Mireuil-sur-Seine, a little corner of the suburbs that you know well.

At that time a German colleague, Julius Hazemann, came to install a mysterious workshop in the heart of that pleasant area, previously consecrated to placid holidaymakers, in which he intended to resolve the big question of the capitation of the radioactivity distributed in nature.

High tension German bluff, what! Which didn't prevent my natural scientific curiosity being excited to white heat, and I resolved to see the man first—an old bear, it was said, absolutely unapproachable—and his machines afterwards.

One day, therefore, I rang at the door of the detached habitation adjacent to the electric workshop. When the door opened I climbed to the first floor and found myself face to face with a charming woman, very young, the wife of Hazemann's son, a coxcomb who was reputed in the vicinity to be a cretin and an accomplished libertine, whereas his father, old Julius, was at least a veritable laborer and a solid scientist.

"Monsieur Carlier, isn't it," said the pretty young lady, smiling at me very amiably. And before I had time to open my mouth, divining as if by a miracle what had brought me, she added: "I fear, unfortunately, that you can't see my father-in-law; it's the hour of his siesta, which is sacred for me, Monsieur Hazemann sleeping very little by night. All the same, since you insist"—I had made a vague gesture, more of courteous protestation—"I'll go into his study on tiptoe, and if, by chance, he isn't asleep..."

She came back, seemingly confused, her lips barred by a vertical finger that seemed to be saying "Shh!" while she made me a sign with her free hand to follow her. In her wake I went along a long semicircular corridor, at the end of which she stopped in front of a glazed bay set back in an angle of the wall and made me a sign to look through the gap in the curtains.

A man was sitting at a tale, his forehead inclined in his hand and his eyes half-closed, who seemed to be meditating or somnolent. I recognized, without hesitation, the white hair, the vast forehead of a thinker, and the energetic features, recently popularized by photographs, of Julius Hazemann.

It only remained for me to withdrew, excusing myself, which I did incontinently, while Madame Hazemann deplored my disappointment in terms of exquisite urbanity.

I went back the following day, and the day after, at a different hour each time, without being any more fortunate. Monsieur Hazemann ended up by sending word to me that he felt that one could not be more touched by my persistence, but that he feared that he would not have the pleasure of making my acquaintance very soon, because of a recent experiment he had instituted, which risked taking up his every minute for some weeks to come, in consequence of which he begged me no longer to take the trouble to disturb myself for some time.

I did not persist that day, but, piqued by the game, I took the road to the workshop again the following Sunday.

This time, I was received by young Hazemann. He started to laugh like a young lunatic on learning about my van attempts to see his father.

"What a specimen, that Julius, eh? Even I, his son, can only see him at long intervals, at meal times…and not then during his crises of gestation, like the one he's going through at the moment." And to his wife, who had just arrived: "Well, is he approachable this morning?"

"Less than ever; for two days the maid and I have only been communicating with him by sliding pieces of paper under the door—but this morning, he doesn't even reply."

"Are you sure," I asked, "that it isn't a case of depression or overwork?"

"A brain as powerful as his," sad Julius's daughter-in-law, biting her lip, "is incapable of any weakness. Anyway, come and see for yourself, as you did the other day."

She and I took the route of the famous semicircular corridor again, and, looking through the gap in the curtains of the bay window, I perceived, as I had the first time, the white-haired head of old Julius, who was still leaning on his elbows, in the slightly outré attitude of Rodin's Thinker.

"No, you see," the young woman commented, "it's certain that he'll only resume his relations with the outside world when the great problem that he's working on is solved.

This time, I confess, I suspected some criminal mystery—who knows, perhaps a monstrous arbitrary

sequestration—and I swore privately to reach the unfortunate old man anyway.

The next day, having kept watch for the departure
of the son for Paris and seen his wife and the maid busy
at the bottom of the garden, I slipped into the house, and
in the blink of a eye was on the staircase, holding my
breath and walking on tiptoe.

Having arrived on the first floor I recognized to my
right, almost immediately, the famous corridor at the
turning of which the scientist's study was situated. My
heart was hammering, because I perceived all too clearly
the disappointing or terrible risks attached to my enterprise. A domestic might surge forth, the door of the
study might be locked or bolted, the scientist might not
be there; there was every chance that he had anticipated
a surprise and taken measures to alert himself by the
most summary means.

Having reached the recessed bay window without
encumbrance, I first observed that the gap in the curtains
had not varied since my first visit; it was sufficient to
permit the perception of the whole room.   Bending
down, I advanced, crawling, in such a fashion as to find
myself directly below the gap; then I raised myself up
progressively, and when my head had surpassed the level of the wood paneling I stuck my eye to the glass.

Julius Hazemann was still sitting at his desk, his
forehead in his hands, his back almost turned to the window, in the same posture as the day before. That appeared to me to be very strange.

I lifted up a door-curtain that surely dissimulated
the entrance to the room. A copper doorknob gleamed in
the penumbra; my feverish hand seized it, but the handle
resisted all my efforts; the door was locked from the inside. What should I do?

For a moment I had the idea of breaking the glass of the bay. What more would I be risking? My irruption into the study, no matter how it was produced, already constituted an unpardonable violation of the laws of hospitality.

And once again, who knew whether the unfortunate old man had not simply been sequestered by his son? It was a hypothesis less and less implausible, at any rate, which simultaneously resolved the enigma of his attitude and legitimated my intervention, even arbitrary and brutal.

I was about to decide in favor of the break-in when, having examined the doorknob at close range I perceived immediately underneath it a cylinder in the form of a navel, like those of electric locks.

I knew the secret of those sorts of locks, but a nervous tremor had seized me, so violent that I took nearly a minute to discover the propitious commutator.

Finally the cylinder allowed the familiar click to be heard in my ear.

I stopped on the threshold of the door, now open, compressing my heartbeats with one hand. The scientist had not budged, and an unspeakable terror finally gripped me on finding myself so close to that grim genius, who had the pretention of discovering and domesticating the secret of all movement and all life.

Was he dreaming, was he asleep? At all hazard, it was important to signify my presence to him without procrastination.

The thick carpet that covered the parquet stifled the four paces I took in order to approach him. I placed my hand on his shoulder; the fabric that my fingers touched was cold—a strange cold that I would not have expected to feel on contact with a garment covering a warm body.

The old man had not budged. An increasing terror rose within me, at the same time as a flood of frightful ideas whirled in my brain. It was necessary now for me to see the face of that man, to see it immediately.

Without hesitation this time, I seized the wrists of the two hands in which the face of the scientist was partly buried...

A terrible shock, the ground disappearing from under my feet, the atrocious fear of losing consciousness, of becoming the living prey of rhythmic force, of isochronic waves, which claws me, corrodes me, carburizes me from head to foot...

My body is bent over that of the nameless, lifeless being, of which I cannot let go, my fingernails digging into the soft wax, increasingly soft, of its wrists—a prodigy simultaneously terrifying and grotesque; I sense it melting beneath me, I see it flowing through the sleeves of the jacket; the forehead, still encrusted in the hands, weeps greasy yellow tears, the white horsehair mane bristles with crackling sparks that spray my face...

Meanwhile, a frenetic bell rings in the wall behind us, vibrating in the drapes, fluttering and swirling in the four corners of the study—the voice of the malevolent genius in the claws of which the mannequin and I are writhing.

I no longer have any but one hope: perhaps someone will hear the bell and come to our rescue; perhaps the wax of the mannequin will melt sufficiently to permit me to release the contact before my heart has cased beating.

I can no longer breathe, nor call out, nor move, and minutes go by like that...at least, I have the impression that they are minutes, but the notion of duration evidently no longer exists for me. At any rate, I have conserved all my presence of mind. My lucidity is even such that I suddenly remember a notice by the engineer Gutman, who found himself abruptly placed, in his laboratory by virtue of the unexpected closure of a switch, in a high tension circuit: an accident that had permitted him subsequently to publicize the sensations received by an electrocuted individual.

My suffering was an homage rendered to the sincerity of the writer. Like him, I perceived the approach of every electric wave, the infinite and regular accumulation of vibrant waves coming from far away, which traversed me, shaking me like a cork floating on a rough sea. Only, the thought of what was going to happen afterwards did not even occur to me, any more than the desire to have the slightest explanation of the colossal trap in which I had just been caught.

Abruptly, everything ceased, the world was put back in place. The door that I had left open behind me had just closed. The mannequin, faceless now, the head singed and the arms half-melted, escaped my hands. I straightened up and encountered the haughty and cold gaze of young Hazemann, who was standing before me, arms folded, in the attitude of an administrator of justice.

He was extraordinarily transfigured by the harsh crease that barred his forehead, the willful arc that finally repudiated the stupid smile, the slack grimaces and the whole mask of puerility and snobbery sported until then. The masculine figure of the man surged forth from behind the fallen mask, the profile of domination and struggle, the interior flame of the gaze hardened by a bitter will to triumph—all that was in a being never seen before, an unsuspected being, of whom I was suddenly almost afraid.

"I couldn't let you die there," the young man said to me, coldly, "but I wonder with what objective you have violated the laws of hospitality..."

I excused myself by telling him frankly the absurd fears that had assailed me. He started to laugh, and his wife, who had arrived, associated herself with his gaiety. Then, very crestfallen, I asked in my turn whether I could pose a question, and they acquiesced.

"With what objective have you imagined the comedy of the mannequin?"

"Old Julius Hazemann no longer exists," replied the young man. "I am the only scientist who bears that name. But the character of Julius, the white-haired scientist, invisible, intangible and inaccessible was imposed upon me by the goal that I am pursuing: the domination of the brute forces of nature—in a word, the domination of the universe itself. A sure instinct had informed me a long time ago of my absolute lack of esthetic prestige. It isn't in my paltry silhouette that the truly great man that I dreamed of imposing on the entire world could be incarnate. I therefore invented old Julius Hazemann, in order to enable him to assume all the grandeurs that await and certainly surpass my own stature."

"All the same," Carlier concluded, "admit that the young man wasn't banal."

THE DIABOLICAL AUTOMOBILE

Is it necessary to add to the rumors according to which Hindu agitators, those who claim to be undermining at the base the colossal Anglo-Indian Empire, have, for some time, had Occidental scientists for auxiliaries accused of delivering to mysterious and formidable engines of destruction to the revolutionaries?

At any rate, this is the terrifying story that was told to us yesterday by the engineer Tarnier on his return from the Far East.

That day, at Z***, on one of the most beautiful islands of English Malaysia, a famous agitator by the name of Tjogang had been arrested. It was decided to summon him the following day before a special investigation committee, but when the bearer of the summons presented himself at the prison, the bird had flown.

The director of the house of detention was literally astounded by that discovery, which he was far from expecting, for, the previous evening, affirmed the guard committed to the surveillance of the prisoner, the later had taken his habitual nourishment and had lain down as usual, without anything allowing the supposition that he was preparing an escape attempt.

The escape itself, moreover, remained so utterly inexplicable that it could by rights appear supernatural.

A summary examination of the location established, in fact, that the detainee could not have disappeared by natural means.

There was no secret exit in the room where he was lodged, the only door of which opened to a gallery to which no one had access. That door had been duly bolted during the escape, and the lock, closed with a double turn, presented no trace of breakage. In addition, the little room had no fireplace, and its two windows and floor were perfectly intact.

It was recognized, on the other hand, on examining the closure of the windows, that they had not been opened for several days. Furthermore, as those windows, situated on a high floor, opened over a flower garden, traces of trodden grass would have been found at the foot of the wall, and footprints n the damp soil, but nothing of the sort existed.

The mystery this remained definitively insoluble, and there was a veritable panic in that beautiful English possession when that new cause of apprehension arrived to add to all those that had been preoccupying minds for some time.

"Oh, if we only had a Sherlock Holmes or a Nick Carter!" said some naïve individuals abused by the reading of popular fiction. But alas, Sherlock Holmes would have lost his Latin in the presence of phenomena that not only surpassed any human conception, but by virtue of their mysterious character, escaped all serious control.

Suddenly, it was learned that coolies had seen the agitator fleeing into the mountains, where all trace of him had been lost.

An expedition was decided by the governor of the island, Lord Cooper, who had promised to end the troubles once and for all, which risked removing all security from the English colonists.

It is necessary to say here that the governor was a model family msn. Not only was he an exemplary husband, attentive and devoted to his slightly unhealthy wife, but he adored his two daughters, Maud and Letty, eighteen and twenty years old—especially Letty, the elder, because she reproduced, at a distance of twenty years, the slender silhouette and tender features of Lady Cooper, who, alas, scarcely resembled herself any more, emaciated as she was by fevers and the hot climate.

Maud was even pettier, with her golden hair and her dazzling complexion, but she had, according to her father, something brisk, almost masculine, about her, by virtue of which she resembled him too much, and distanced her in consequence from his feminine ideal.

Maud did not seem to be discomfited in the least by her own petulance and the ardor that brooded within her, giving the impression of a poorly tamed colt; was it not thanks to her exuberant temperament that she had been able to resist the depressing influence of that fiery sky, avoiding the anemia that had corroded her mother and was etiolating her sister in the flower of her youth? Her young breast swelled beneath the brightly-colored langouti;[16] she inhaled life through all the pores of her fresh and flowery skin; she embraced the future, life and the entire world with a bright and dominating gaze, in which the slightest details of the exotic frame that contained her were reflected.

It was also with that gaze that she was now contemplating her fiancé, who had just come in. The young captain, Harry Worth, inclined before the governor, making the military salute; then he kissed Lady Cooper's wrist and made as if to sit down—but Maud was already drawing him into a corner.

---

[16] This is odd, as the term langouti usually refers to a loincloth.

"The detachment is ready," he had time to murmur into the governor's ear. "We'll depart tomorrow at dawn."

"And I'll accompany you," Maud added, almost in his ear, as soon as they were isolated at the other end of the veranda.

"It's very bad on the part of little girls," growled the young captain, "to spy on military secrets."

"First of all, I'm not a little girl," replied Maud, laughing. "I'm almost as tall as you."

And that was true, even though Captain Harry was a fine figure of a man.

"Secondly, your secrets are known all over town, for everyone knows that at sunrise tomorrow morning, a cavalry column is being launched in pursuit of this Tjogang, who has taken refuge in the mountains."

The captain twisted his blond moustache without replying. A confusion burst forth in his martial face that rendered it even dearer to Maud. Harry was also elegant and well-built, and wore his uniform delightfully.

The young woman touched his arm. "You'll take me won't you? she murmured, imploringly.

"The governor will oppose it."

"My father does everything I wish."

And that was so true that when Maud declared before everyone that she would go with the expeditionary column, Lord Cooper protested energetically, but gave as a reason for his formal refusal that he did not see a horse she could mount—with the result that the following morning, when Maud appeared, fully equipped, on a young chestnut mare that was her father's own, the governor could only raise his arms in a sign of distress, repeating several times: "Oh, well then...oh, well then..."

The expeditionary platoon was already lined up in the court of honor of the summer palace. They were superb Malabars with frizzy black beards and heads coiffed in vast white turbans. Their curved sabers where glittering in the sunlight and their burnooses fell in noble folds over the rumps of their wiry and spirited little horses.

At a curt command they set forth, with a young lieutenant at their head who knew the mountains like the back of his hand.

Captain Harry and his pretty fiancée brought up the rear, the latter never ceasing to wave her handkerchief in the direction of the veranda on which Lord and Lady Cooper were leaning, with their elder daughter Letty, pale with anxiety—for the two sisters adored one another, in spite of their dissimilar characters.

It was a splendid spring morning, which further heightened the charm and beauty of the terrestrial paradise of the Anglo-Malaysian island. The route followed by the column was all pink, a pomegranate pink, and snaked among the plantations of tea and quinquina, intercut by mountain streams and waterfalls, groves of coconut palms, palm trees and monstrous ferns.

At a bend, snowy peaks stacked up their imposing masses against the sky, to a height of three thousand meters. One might have thought it a landscape of the Swiss or Tyrolean Alps.

After two hours of riding, the little troop reached the entrance to a somber defile opening like a saber-but in the granite mass of the mountain. The captain recommended his platoon to advance slowly, with the greatest prudence. Two riders scouted the route, pistols high the rest followed two hundred meters behind, three abreast.

They had been marching in that order for a quarter of an hour when the two scouts suddenly fell back, galloping toward their comrades.

"Well, what is it?" asked Harry's second-in-command, a lieutenant.

They said that they had heard a formidable rumble in the distance, a noise like nothing they had ever heard before, and which was approaching rapidly.

Captain Harry arrived and lent a ear. His fiancée saw him pale slightly.

"That's singular," he murmured. "One might think it were the rhythmic purr of an automobile, but a monstrous automobile, for the noise is truly that of thunder on the march."

Maud could hear it now, and she raised her binoculars in order to inspect the depths of the defile, which extended as far as the eye could see, at a shallow slope, between the two vertical walls of the gorge.

"Strange," she murmured, "that an automobile can risk such a route."

Suddenly, a cry escaped the breast of the lieutenants, whose eyes were searching the narrow perspective of that tunnel of sorts.

"A black dot, increasing in size with unusual speed!"

All eyes followed his gesture.

A somber machine was racing from the depths of the horizon with lighting rapidity, blocking the sky, occupying the entire width of the defile.

"Look out!" shouted the lieutenant to the men, and an instant later, as the infernal machine arrived upon them like a bolide, he shouted again, and they were his last words:

"Get down!"

"Bah!" said Maud, insouciantly. "They only have to stand still."

But the cavaliers had obeyed, having leapt to the ground or plastered themselves against the walls of the defile. Even Captain Harry had done likewise.

Only Maud had remained upright in the saddle, as if to bar the route to the unleashed monster.

Then something unusual happened.

The machine arrived in a whirlwind, with an infernal roar. One might have thought it a living cyclone.

Maud only just had time to see two men sitting at the steering-wheel: an indigene, the famous Tjogang, and a European, an old man with a grave and sad expression.

The front of the vehicle reared up, showing the underside of its chassis.

The horses of the avant-garde collapsed, knocked over by the squall, and the young lieutenant disappeared, carried away like a wisp of straw.

Frightened, Maud curbed her back, and sensed a burning breath above her head. Then she straightened up, astonished to be still alive.

The machine had just made a terrible bound, leaping over the fragile obstacle that the young amazon presented to it, without touching her.

Captain Harry remained as if incrusted against the wall of rock. He had not received any wound, but he was as pale as a dead man. Swiftly, he launched himself toward Maud. The fantastic automobile was far away now, but around the captain and the fiancée one might have thought there was a battlefield. Half a dozen horses had been decapitated, their heads scythed off at the level of the withers. Cavaliers were writhing, bloodied, mad with terror.

The engineer Tarnier, to whom Maud Cooper recounted this story herself, is still wondering whether the young woman and her fiancé were not victims on this occasion of a frightful hallucination. The only certain thing is that the expeditionary platoon had been cruelly decimated by a diabolical engine of locomotion of which no one could describe the exact form.